Dom's Ascension

#1 IN THE MARIANI CRIME FAMILY SERIES

By

HARLEY
STONE

Dom's Ascension is a work of fiction. Names, characters, places, and incidents are the products of the author's imagination and are used fictitiously. Any resemblance to actual events, locales, or persons, living or dead, is entirely coincidental.

ISBN: 978-1979907569
2017 Harley Stone
Copyright © 2017 by Harley Stone
All rights reserved.

Published in the United States

ACKNOWLEDGMENTS

Special thanks to my husband, Meltarrus, our boys, and all my friends and family for understanding when my mind is tied up in a fictional reality, and to all my amazing beta readers who pointed out edits and encouraged me through the process.

Thank you, Jackson Jackson, for your fantastic cover design wizardry!

Dedicated to:
my bestie, Piper, who doesn't let anyone get in my way...
especially not me.
Thanks for your steadfast friendship, your brutal honesty,
and your unwavering support.
I love you!

CHAPTER ONE
Dominico

March 7, 1992

*I*T WAS SATURDAY night and I'd been hustling since early morning. With my sights fixed on the black Porsche 911 in front of me, anticipating the party it would soon drive me to, I almost got my ass handed to me in the parking lot of my father's casino.

Thankfully, my friend, Mario, had my back and was paying attention. "Heads up, Dom, we've got company," he whispered, nodding behind us before slipping away.

Head down, I kept walking, pretending not to notice the two sets of footsteps closing in on me. It would take a special kind of stupid mother-fucker to believe he could jump me on my own turf.

"Hey you, hold up!"

I recognized the fake southern drawl of the cowboy from tonight's poker game. At least it wasn't one of the rival families. Just some *chooch*—some moron—in search of his pride after Mario and I had cleaned out his wallet during the game.

Taking a deep breath, I halted my steps and spun around to surprise them with an attack. A fist came flying at my face, not connected to the cowboy from tonight's game. I didn't recognize the attacker, who was all corded muscle with a thick-neck and a hard expression. Probably in his late thirties, a thug hired to intimidate, but didn't know how to fight. He'd overcommitted to the punch and when I dodged, he lost his balance. Before he could recover, I countered with an uppercut, striking the bottom of his chin with a crunch, ringing his bell good for him.

In the seconds it took him to get his bearings, I stepped back and scanned the area. The wannabe cowboy, Dean Jones, watched from the opposite side of a silver sedan. Wearing a black felt cowboy hat, a teal western shirt with honest-to-god ruffles, and a shit-eating grin, Dean was so busy watching the fight he didn't see Mario circling back around.

Not wanting to draw attention to my sneaking friend, I turned back to the hired thug. He raised his fists like some sort of boxer and came at me again. Did he expect me follow suit? Like I'd be stupid enough to box someone twice my size. Not hardly. I kicked him in the kneecap. His body bucked to the side and he limped a step backwards, mouth gaping open as he stared at me like I'd broken some cardinal rule. I laughed, enjoying myself. The bastard had jumped me in a casino parking lot and expected me to fight fair? I was about to show him a thing or two about fighting dirty when the sound of a round being chambered drew my attention.

Mario had never been a fighter, claiming his hands were far too valuable to be busting up faces. My friend was possibly the best card shark in all of Vegas, with a sleight of hand that even the Pope would call a gift. Because he didn't fight, Mario always came heavy and never hesitated to draw. He pressed the business end of his Glock 19 against Dean's side. The hired thug limped another step back and raised his hands in surrender.

"Easy there," Dean said to Mario. "We're just messin' with the kid."

"Messin' with me? I'm disappointed in you, Dean." I tutted. "Having your guard dog jump me from behind? Fuckin' coward. You should have come at me yourself, and from the front, like you had some balls."

"It's the jeans," Mario said. "My god, they're so tight I bet you can't even bend over. Probably cut off the blood flow and shriveled his twig and berries right up."

Dean looked from me to Mario. "I knew that game was fixed."

It wasn't a question, so Dean must have had at least two brain cells to rub together after all. Of course Uncle Carlo's "executive poker game" was fixed. Only the high rollers with more money than power and brains were invited. The buy-in was three grand, the drinks were strong, and the servers were built and dressed to distract while we ran the table. Mario played the part of some dumb kid who'd come to town to blow his newly-received inheritance, and I pretended to be the bored son of a traveling tycoon. I'm sure most of the losers knew they'd been played, but sucked down their free cocktails and slunk back to their room to lick their wounds and reinvest whatever cash we'd let them walk away with. Rarely did anyone hire muscle and come after us.

"Oh no, Dom. We got a real scholar on our hour hands. What should we do?" Mario asked.

I chuckled and patted both men down. Dean had a knife in his pocket but was otherwise clean. His associate had a pistol. I pocketed the knife and released the safety on the gun before pointing it at my attacker.

"Just give me back the money you stole and we'll be on our way," Dean said. "I won't even rat you out to the other players or the casino management."

Mario and I had their guns, and the dipshit was threatening us? I laughed. "Cowboy, you're in no position to negotiate, and your money is long gone."

Funds were allocated even before the poker game started. My father—our family boss—took his cut off the top. Next came Uncle Carlo's management fee. He was the family underboss, or second in command. Incidentals and staff were paid, and then the remainder was split between me and Mario. The two of us had each walked away with a little over five grand. It was a drop in the bucket compared to the thirty-three large we'd lifted from Dean and the rest of the shmucks at the table, and there was no way he would get a dollar of it back. Especially not while Mario and I held him and his crony at gunpoint.

"Don't be stupid, kid," Dean warned. "You know I'm loaded. Lots of resources. I'll find you and take back what you owe me."

"He's got a point, Dom," Mario said. "Maybe we should just shoot him so we don't have to worry about it."

Most people underestimated Mario. Shy of six feet tall with a wiry build, his stature didn't exactly strike fear into the heart of anyone. But his eyes were another story. Something terrifying raged deep within and when Mario got pissed, you could look into his eyes and see your death.

Dean must have seen it now, because he paled.

Good. It was time to let him know who he was dealing with. We weren't some punk kids; we ran this city. Or, at least, we would someday. I glanced at my watch counting down the valuable minutes of free time I had remaining. Damn this idiot for keeping me from a much-needed good time. "No time. We've got a party to get to, remember?"

"Can we call someone to clean up the mess for us?" Mario asked. "Anyone in the family owe you a favor?"

Dean cut his eyes back and forth between us a couple times, and then he guffawed. "The family? That's rich. Just because you're Italian, you expect me to believe you're part of some mafia family? Everybody knows the FBI chased the mobsters out of Vegas more than a decade ago."

Everyone knew what the mafia and the FBI wanted them to know. It helped common people sleep at night and politicians get reelected.

"We gotta do somethin' with them," Mario said, jabbing his pistol into Dean's side. "Any ideas?"

We were toward the back of the parking lot, but I still didn't want to chance being seen holding two idiots at gunpoint. That was almost as bad for business as leaving bodies lying around. Dean was a guest of the casino and loaded enough to buy friends who would miss him if he didn't make it home. And my old man would kick my ass if I brought a police investigation to the doorstep of his casino.

I gestured for Mario to follow me with Dean as I led his thug to the back entrance of the casino. I beat on the door until it swung open, and a soldier by the name of Dag filled the doorway. Dag stood about six feet tall and was three hundred-plus pounds of pure muscle. He had the jowls of a bulldog and the legs of a horse. I knew, because I'd been kicked by him while in training. Since his size and constant scowl frightened the guests, Carlo kept him stationed by the back door, which meant Dag spent most nights underutilized and bored out of his mind.

"Yeah?" the big man barked.

I stepped aside so he could see the men behind me. "Mario and I are running late for a…a meeting, and these two tried to jump us." I pulled a hundred-dollar bill out of my pocket. "I'd deal with 'em myself, but I don't got time, so I'd appreciate it if you could set 'em straight for me."

Dag grinned, and I had to force myself not to wince. His eyes lit up as he took my cash and stuffed it in his pocket. Then his two meaty paws reached past me, landing on a shoulder of each of the men. He yanked them forward and shoved them into the casino. "You betcha."

"Thanks, Dag. I owe you one."

His grin widened. "You don't owe me shit, Dom. I'm lookin' forward to this."

"Nothing above the shoulders. They're guests, and you know how Carlo gets when guests come hobbling in with their faces all busted up. But make sure you let 'em know what happens if they try to rat us out."

Dag gave me a hard look, conveying that he knew how to do his job, and then the door closed.

My old man would beat my ass good if he found out I'd shirked my responsibility like that, but I rarely got a night off. I should be half-wasted with a girl on each knee by now. Besides, I'd just made Dag's night and knew he wouldn't go waggin' his jaw.

"All right," I said, pocketing the stolen gun and palming my car keys. "Let's hit that party."

As we walked away from the door, I wondered how much damage Dag would have to do before the cowboy realized the mob will always run Vegas.

CHAPTER TWO
Annetta

"THIS IS IT, Papa, the one I've been looking for," I said, highlighting the help wanted ad. "Chef needed ASAP, knowledge of classic Italian dishes a must, come prepared to cook. None of that "prior experience necessary" nonsense. This has my name all over it!"

Papa smiled down at me, patting the back of my head, patronizing me with a kind gesture. At twenty-one, and freshly graduated from the Culinary Academy, I was in search of my first full-time job, not six and excited about being a butterfly in the school play. And I needed this, since the part-time grocery clerk position I'd held since high school wasn't exactly a cocoon I could grow my wings in.

"I thought we decided you were going back to school first," Papa said.

Here we go again.

Fighting the urge to roll my eyes, I reminded him of our last conversation about my future. "I love you, Papa, but I've passed all my classes and I have glowing recommendations from my instructors. I'm not going back to school. What I need now, is a real job so I can start paying off the loans you took out to make that happen."

"You let me worry about the loans while you focus on getting the best education you can." He picked up the University of Nevada Las Vegas course catalog, which conveniently kept finding its way to our kitchen table, and thumbed through it like he didn't have the whole thing memorized. "I know you want to cook, *luce dei miei occhi.*"

Light of my eyes. The Italian term of endearment was sweet, and I'd always appreciated it, but lately it felt like Papa's love for me was leaving him blind.

"*Want* to cook? Papa it's much more than that. This is my dream, and I'm good at it, you know I am. You promised you'd support me in this."

He sighed. "I know, and I do."

Hearing the hesitancy in his tone, I eyed him, waiting for the "but."

Instead, he let out another long, drawn-out sigh, finally relenting. "You're right, it sounds like a great opportunity." He plucked the phone from its wall base, untangling the cord as he held it out to me. "Call them and request an interview."

Since I was an adult, I didn't need my father's permission, but knowing I had his support made me feel like I could leap over even the tallest of hurdles. And no work history in the food industry had been an ankle-breaker for sure. I needed a little pep talk to get through this.

"It says come ready to cook. If I could just get the opportunity to prepare some dishes for them…"

"You'll not only get the job, you'll win over their hearts as well."

I accepted the phone, his endorsement giving me the courage I needed to make the call.

*   *   *

The chef position was at Antonio's, one of two five-star Italian restaurants in Vegas. Unable to contain my excitement, I practically pranced all the way from the bus stop and through the mahogany and glass doors, before skidding to a stop. Shy of nine thirty a.m., the restaurant wasn't open yet, giving me the chance to gawk at its beauty in peace. I'd spent my entire life in Vegas, but had never seen the inside of Antonio's. Dinner here wasn't exactly in our family budget. Crystal chandeliers hung over mahogany tables draped with red and white checkered tablecloths to maintain the Italian feel. Pristine hardwood floors were accented with classy rugs that played off the colors in the drapes, the dark upholstered booths, and the custom moldings. I could almost picture my dishes on the table, placed before salivating guests who were ready to give us raving reviews. It was exactly the fine dining experience I'd dreamed of being a part of.

"Can I help you?" someone asked.

I snapped my jaw closed and turned to find the suited maître d' watching me, his lips turned up in amusement.

Feeling shabby and underdressed in my standard white chef coat and pinstriped pants, with my hair pulled back in a bun and a backpack of my mother's old recipes slung over my shoulder, it was an effort to keep my back straight and my chin up.

Confidence, Annetta, pretend you belong here.

"Hi." I gave him my friendliest smile. "I'm here to interview for the job. The chef job."

He nodded at my clothes. "I gathered that. Résumé?"

I opened my backpack and pulled one out for him.

He looked it over then nodded. "You're early. Stay here and I'll check and see if they're ready for you."

He drifted behind a mirrored wall, leaving me in the entrance with no clue what to do with myself. I picked up a menu and scanned the salads, appetizers, and entrées. There were a few dishes I didn't recognize, but for the most part nothing sounded too difficult. The menu had room for additions, and I allowed myself to dream about adding a couple of my specialties. And removing a few of theirs.

"Fettuccini Alfredo? Seriously? It's not even Italian."

I smacked a hand over my mouth and glanced around, thankfully still alone. Nobody wanted the opinions of a freshly graduated chef with zero experience. Especially not before I got the job. Sliding the menu back onto the stack, I leaned against a booth and kept my mouth shut as I waited.

Three other people dressed in chef coats showed, clustering around me as they checked out the restaurant. The maître d' returned and showed us to an immaculate kitchen full of stainless steel industrial appliances. A few chefs were working on food prep, but we stepped around them and were each assigned to an empty station. A silver-haired stocky man with a slight overbite laid down his knife and turned to address us.

"Hello. My name is Frank. I'm one of the chefs here and I've been asked to explain the duties of the position. If selected, you'll be responsible for directing the preparation, seasoning, and cooking of all dishes while you're on shift. You'll be expected to participate in the planning and pricing of menu items, the ordering of supplies, and keeping of records and accounts. You'll supervise and participate in cooking, baking, and food prep, as well as the scheduling and monitoring of kitchen personnel. This is not an entry-level position. However, we find ourselves down a chef unexpectedly and need to hire someone today. But only if we find the right candidate."

He paused, and his gaze drifted over us. I got the feeling he wasn't impressed with what he saw. I straightened my shoulders and pasted a smile across my face, refusing to let some monotone who'd obviously memorized his script intimidate me.

"We are aware that sometimes skills speak louder than experience, so management is giving each of you a rare opportunity to impress their taste buds before they look at your résumé. You will be expected to prepare an original Italian entrée, not on our menu."

He then proceeded to show us where all the ingredients were kept before dropping the bombshell. "You have thirty minutes. If you're not done by then, throw your work in the trash and see yourself out to make room for the next round of candidates. If, by some chance, you have created something edible, your dish will be presented to management and you will continue on with the interview process." Frank didn't even give us a chance to ask questions before starting the timer and returning to his station.

The other applicants snapped to work while I stood there staring at the time. Thirty minutes to impress. What could I whip up in thirty minutes that would knock their socks off? Especially in a strange kitchen? I washed my hands and put on gloves while considering the recipes in my backpack. Their presence served as more of a security blanket than a necessity since I had most of Mom's recipes memorized, complete with the revisions I'd made over the years.

My favorite recipe was one I rarely made because the ingredients were expensive. *Linguine di Mare*, linguine of the sea, called for a well-seasoned mix of calamari, mussels, scallops, and shrimp in a garlicy white wine sauce. Assuming I could find everything I needed, I could have the rest of the dish put together in the time it took the noodles to boil. Determined to make it happen, I set a pot of water on the stovetop to boil and got to work.

With four minutes to spare, I handed Frank my offering. He eyeballed it, then me, before grabbing a fork out of the drawer and tasting a sauce-drenched noodle wrapped around a scallop. His eyebrows rose as he chewed. Then, without a single word to me, he turned on his heel and whisked out of the kitchen.

I stared after him for a moment, wondering whether his sudden disappearance was encouraging or damning before remembering that my station was a mess. Turning to clean, I scanned the kitchen.

The applicant across the table from me looked as if she was about to burst into tears. She bent to collect her belongings, casting a furtive glance at the large garbage can at the end of the stations before heading out the way we'd entered. Curious, I took my scraps to the trash and peeked in.

"He took one bite and had her toss the whole thing," said one of the two male applicants, his own entrée plated in his hands and ready for Frank to evaluate.

I felt bad for the girl, but happy for myself. At least Frank hadn't trashed my meal. That would be humiliating, and I probably would have told him off. Wondering what gave Frank the right to be such a bully, I finished scrubbing down my station.

When Frank returned, he took the man's dish.

The buzzer went off.

Frank looked past us to the second male applicant, who was still working on his creation. "Throw it away and see yourself out," Frank snapped before disappearing again, plate still in hand.

The applicant didn't even bother to clean up after himself before storming out, leaving only two of us.

We didn't have to wait long before Frank returned and extended one long finger toward the other remaining applicant. "You, come with me."

I didn't even get the chance to ask him what I should do before Frank disappeared again.

"Good luck," I whispered as the other applicant followed Frank.

"If you're looking for something to do, there are some onions there that need to be chopped."

I turned, looking for the owner of the voice, to find a thin, nice-looking blond man watching me. He couldn't have been much older than I was, but his steely-blue eyes made him look too intense for his age. He nodded toward the onions in front of him before returning his attention to the chicken he was chopping.

Wondering if this was some sort of test to see if I was a team player or whatever, I washed my hands again, put on fresh gloves, and scooped up the first onion.

"The waiting's the worst," he said. "I'm Brandon, by the way."

"Annetta." I set the onion down on the board and grabbed a knife. "The other guy is being interviewed, right?"

It seemed like the obvious answer to his disappearance, but the restaurant management desperately needed to work on its communication.

"Yes," Brandon replied, going about his work.

"Well, that's reassuring, because I'm kinda picking up an ax murderer vibe from that Frank character."

Brandon chuckled.

Realizing I'd let my thoughts tumble out of my mouth, I shook my head at myself. "Sorry. I probably shouldn't have said that."

He beamed me a smile. "I won't tell anyone. Besides, Frank's not too bad. Just intense."

Keeping one eye on the door, I finished the onions and started crushing garlic. Frank returned and motioned me back, barely giving me enough time to remove my gloves and grab my bag before he disappeared again. Running to catch up, I turned the corner and stumbled to a stop inside a big office with a long table down the center. Four men sat at the table, watching my ungracious entry. The first stood and introduced himself as Collin Royal, the restaurant manager. The other three offered only first names with no titles.

"You're a chef?" the suited man named Dominico asked, eyebrows shooting up his forehead with surprise. Bloodshot eyes watched me from under dark, messy hair as he cradled his head like it hurt. He was attractive, and I would have felt bad for his obvious pain, but both his question and tone rankled. I'd worked extremely hard to earn my title and didn't appreciate his obvious skepticism. Assuming he was just another pig-headed chauvinist, I raised my chin and said, "Yes sir. They're letting women in these days."

It wasn't the wisest choice of words for a prospective employee, but if he was half as sexist as his comment suggested, I'd never make it past my first week here anyway.

Forget the beautiful restaurant and perfect kitchen. Might as well torch the opportunity now than wait and ruin my work history with an early termination.

Seated beside Dominico, Mario snickered.

Dominico's mouth twitched, but he didn't back down. "What I meant is that you're very beautiful. Seems a shame to hide you away in a kitchen."

My cheeks burned with both anger and embarrassment. Was he trying to flatter me during my interview? I needed a job and this handsome player seemed insistent on blowing it for me. I'd had enough. "My apologies sir. I didn't mean to misrepresent, but all the ugly women are currently becoming meter maids and mail clerks."

This time Dominico cracked a smile. It lit up his entire face and made my breath catch. No matter how big of a pig he was, the man was downright gorgeous when he smiled.

Mario leaned forward. "The dish you prepared was excellent. It's your own recipe?"

Thankful for the change of topic, I took a breath. "My mother's, but I altered it."

"Perhaps it's your mother we should be interviewing," Michael suggested. My attention turned to him, noting the resemblance he shared with Dominico. I'd bet my best spatula the two were related, with not an ounce of manners to spare between them.

"That would be impossible, since she's dead."

Even though I hadn't had many interviews, I was pretty certain this one was a flop. Michael clamped his mouth shut and Mario looked away. Nobody apologized for the crass statement, but they did manage to seem uncomfortable if not embarrassed.

Finally, Collin stepped in. "Legally speaking, you own your mother's recipes then, correct?"

"Yes, and I have made my own alterations for each one. I attended the Culinary Academy of Las Vegas and earned—"

"Yes, we have your résumé," he said, waving it in the air. "If we need anything else, we'll call."

And with that, I was dismissed. Frank shooed me out a back exit, the door clicking shut behind me.

"Well, I'm never going to hear from them again. Good riddance, *luridi porci*," I muttered as I headed for the bus stop. "Filthy pigs!"

A group of tourists looked at me like I was crazy, but I didn't care. I didn't need Antonio's. There were lots of opportunities for experience-less cooks like myself. My throat constricted just thinking the lie. I'd almost talked myself into believing I didn't even want the job when Collin called the next day and shocked me to my core with an offer.

I probably should have turned him down.

CHAPTER THREE
Dominico

"𝒮HE'S PERFECT," I said, the minute Frank escorted the beautiful, fiery brunette out of the office.

Michael snorted. "Perfect for your bedroom, maybe."

"No, perfect for the position," I replied.

Michael shook his head. "If you weren't so damn hung over you'd be able to see what a nightmare she'd be. Tell him, Mario."

Michael's words were way too loud. I winced and took another sip of water, hoping it would help. Last night's rager had sent me stumbling home somewhere around four a.m. I'd completely forgotten about today's interviews, and still wasn't sure why I had to be a part of them. Mario, I could see being there, since his family owned a restaurant and he occasionally stuck his head in and pretended to manage it. But me? What did I know about hiring anyone? All I knew was Annetta Porro had a damn fine body, a cute face, and could cook. Checked off enough qualifications for me.

Mario snickered. "You always did like the feisty ones, Dom. She seems like trouble. And look at this résumé… no restaurant work history. This caliber of establishment can be very stressful. Especially during an event like your sister's engagement party. What if she can't hang and screws something up?"

"If the dinner's not perfect, the De Luccas will see it as an insult, and we end up in a war with the Durante family without their support," Michael said, his voice booming in my brain. "Is that worth some piece of ass to you, Dom?"

Only Italians would claim offense over a subpar meal. Still, the Durantes were the most powerful family in Vegas, and we needed the support of my sister's future in-laws to take them out and dethrone their don, a sociopath by the name of Maurizio Durante.

"Because if you need to get laid that bad, I know plenty of broads who'll—"

"I get it," I said cutting Michael off. My head hurt far too much to enjoy the normal verbal sparring with my brother. Michael wasn't a bad guy, but as the family heir he had a lot riding on his shoulders, and somewhere along the way his responsibilities had leeched away his sense of humor and turned him into the son our old man loved to brag about. As for me, I was just trying not to be too big of a disappointment.

Mario stood. "I'll go let Frank know we're ready for the next applicant." He headed for the door.

The rest of the day passed in a blur of unimpressive applicants presenting mediocre dishes, none of which held a fork to the enchanting Annetta Porro and her delicious seafood pasta. Despite her lack of experience, the girl had confidence and personality, which convinced me she could handle the stress of the kitchen. Sure, other applicants had more experience, but Annetta clearly had instincts and fire. I kept reminding myself I shouldn't care who got the job. I didn't work at the restaurant. She'd be in the kitchen and I wouldn't even see her at the dinner. In fact, I'd probably never see her again. But for some reason, I did care, and by the time Frank disappeared to let out the last applicant, I was more certain than ever that she was the chef for the job.

"We have to make a decision today," Mario said, thumbing through the stack of résumés.

"You know how I feel about it," I said, leaning back and throwing my hands in the air.

Michael frowned, "We're not hiring someone just because you're sprung on her. Think with your brain and put the family first for a second."

"Whoa." That rankled. I sat up and stared him down. "Yes, she's hot and I would very much like to see what she looks like out of that uniform, but did you taste her dish? It was by far the best. Maybe you should put the family first, and stop blocking her just because I like her."

Michael stiffened.

"Look, you and Father dragged me into this process for some reason, so that's my opinion. We're here to hire the best, and she's it," I said. "This is all about making an impression and showing the De Luccas how much we value their alliance. You honestly think any of those other dishes will impress them?"

He glared at me for a moment before turning to the restaurant manager. "What do you think?" he asked.

The manager—his name was Cain or Connor or something—looked from Michael to me, then down at the résumés. "I-I-I don't want to step on any toes…"

Unsolicited, we were helping him interview chefs for the restaurant he managed, and I hadn't even bothered to learn the guy's name. And he didn't want to step on our toes? Such was the power of my family.

"Then don't," Michael said. "Who would you choose if we weren't here?"

"Um…" He swallowed and studied the résumé on the table in front of him. "Ms. Porro's dish was exquisite, but you bring up a valid point about her work history. She has been working at the same place since high school, though, which does show work ethic and loyalty, but working in a kitchen is different."

"The girl's loyal, Mike," I said. "What's more important to the family than that?"

"Of course, I could be a little biased because Linguine di Mare is my favorite dish," the manager continued, still waffling. "I've had it prepared by some of the finest chefs both here and abroad, but Ms. Porro's version... exquisite, unique, and knowing she owns other such treasures intrigues me greatly. As a businessman and a food enthusiast, I'd love to get my hands on her recipes."

"Okay, so she can cook," Michael reluctantly agreed. "Fine, hire her. But make sure you run a full background check first. If she has any ties to any of the families, I want to know immediately. Bring her in tomorrow and get her trained."

The manager grabbed a pen and jotted down notes.

"Anything to add, Mario?" Michael asked.

Mario nodded. "Stress test her. It won't matter how great her dishes are if she can't handle the pressure. If she fails, all our heads are gonna roll, so be sure you have trained back-ups, just in case."

It seemed unreal that everyone was this keyed up about a goddamn dinner, but that was the way of a rising family. Everything we did had to be thought through and handled correctly, since we needed to prove we were competent and powerful.

With the decision made, Mario and the manager worked out the details while Michael grabbed the office phone and made a call. With nothing to do, I stacked the applications, setting Annetta's on top. Then I memorized her phone number.

When Michael returned to the table he pulled me to the side and let me know one of our warehouses missed their drop and Father wanted us to check it out. And with that it was back to family business as usual.

*   *   *

Mario drove my Porsche home from the restaurant and I slid into the passenger's seat of Michael's black Acura NSX. With its full leather interior and VTEC engine, the NSX was my brother's pride and joy. He revved up the engine to life, and we headed south.

The family owned several warehouses around the city, each one on record under a different fictitious name. It was one of the many ways my old man kept Uncle Sam out of the family coffers. Warehouses were used to process stolen or manufactured goods, and money drops were made one to three times a day, depending on the flow of business. The warehouse in question was currently moving a cocaine ship-ment, so it should be making money drops at least twice dai-ly. Carlo had called to check on them when they missed the evening drop, and nobody answered.

The warehouse was located in a brick building behind a lounge on West Spring Mountain Road, between an imported car lot and a Korean restaurant. An empty lot occupied the land behind it, with a low-income housing development be-yond that.

We drove around the block a couple of times, checking out the scene. It was dinner time, and the restaurant's parking lot was filling up. Six cars were parked in front of the lounge, and traffic at the car lot was dismal. Nothing seemed out of place and no one appeared to be too interested in us or the warehouse, so we pulled into the empty lot and scoped out the building. The security lights were on, but while we wait-ed nobody came or left, which was odd.

I pulled the P229 SIG SAUER from my pocket, checked the magazine, and flicked off the safety. "You ready, Mike?"

At his nod, we slid out of the car. I slipped my weapon back in my pocket but kept my hand on it. Michael beeped his car alarm on as we crossed the lot, heading for the front door. Listening, I heard no sounds other than traffic and the loud rock music of the lounge.

"How do you want to handle this?" I asked, deferring to my older brother.

"Through the front door. Stay by me."

Most mafia bosses wouldn't send their two heirs into a potentially dangerous situation, but our old man made it clear that if we couldn't survive the life, we didn't deserve it. I could see his logic, but still, it would have been nice if he'd at least sent us backup.

The front door stood ajar. We drew our guns and crept in slowly. We'd done this sort of thing over a hundred times, but it still made my heart pound, knowing anyone could be inside waiting to pop us off. We slipped around the corner and pointed our guns, just like we'd been trained to, only there was nobody standing to threaten. Four bullet-ridden bodies were lying on the ground, all of which I recognized.

We stuck together and searched the rest of the warehouse, finding it clear. The blood of the bodies was congealing, so whoever had made the hit was probably long gone by now. Michael swore and lowered his weapon, picking up the receiver of the phone on the countertop. He dialed and put it to his ear while I wandered around the room. Blood was splattered everywhere, and the place reeked of shit. In addition to the gunshot wounds, chunks of clothing and flesh had been flayed off two of the men.

Mobsters often left messages with their hits. A bullet through the eye meant the family who'd ordered the hit was watching. A bullet through the mouth meant the victim had been a snitch. But I'd never heard of a message connected to flaying a person. I dragged a hand down my face and tried to figure out why the hell these two had been tortured. It didn't make any sense.

In the middle of the room stood two empty tables, with a safe in the corner. Michael hung up the phone and made a beeline for the safe. He put in the code and opened it up to reveal a pile of cash.

"At least they didn't get the money," he said, pulling it out and locking the safe back up.

Sometimes my brother sounded eerily like our old man. All these men were dead, and he was proud none of them had given up the code. "Harsh, Mike."

He shrugged. "What do you want me to do, cry for them? Build them a shrine? Sorry, but I don't have time to do any of that shit, because I'm gonna go catch the bastards who did this. Now let's get out of here. Father's calling in a clean-up crew."

He made it sound like they'd be cleaning up trash, or some sort of spill. Not people we knew. Searching for some whisper of humanity in him, I said, "That guy with the gun... he's got a kid. A little girl. She was at dinner a couple of weeks ago, remember?"

"Yeah. This one right here has a wife. You wanna stick around and reminisce? Maybe explain to their families why their killers are still out there? Cool, but I'm gonna go hunt them down."

"Does Father know who did this?" I asked.

Michael cocked his head. "We all know who did this. Let's talk in the car."

We hustled out to his Acura and took off. After we'd put a few blocks between us and the murder scene, Michael filled me in on his conversation with our old man.

"He suspects the Durantes are behind the hit, but wants the names of the men who pulled the triggers. He's given us permission to do whatever it takes to get them."

I knew what that meant. Michael and I spent the rest of the night crashing all the usual hot spots where hitmen were known to wag their jaws while blowing off steam. We paid off whores and bartenders, threatened a few contacts, even dropped a couple ounces of weed as bribes. Other than instilling more fear and respect for our family, we got nothing.

Somewhere around four a.m., during a coffee stop at some dive, Michael's pager went off. After a quick call on the payphone, we were off again. This time Michael drove us to an older bar not far from the strip. We parked on the side and went to the back entrance. Michael knocked out a tune, and a bouncer answered and showed us to a small, cluttered office. He cleared coats off the sofa and invited us to sit. "Tom'll be in in a second," he said after we were situated. A few minutes later, a guy who couldn't have been much older than me and Michael joined us. He took off his apron and tossed it on the desk. "You must be Mike and Dom," he said, shaking our hands. "We spoke on the phone. I'm Tom." With introductions out of the way, Tom leaned against the desk and got right down to business. "One of my regulars was in here tonight... a loud mouth dipshit who goes by the name of Chains. He's always braggin' about one fight or another, and tonight I overheard him sayin' he and a few friends jumped a warehouse. He was all hopped up on coke, so I thought it might be connected."

"Chains?" I asked.

"That's what they call him. I don't know his real name. Always pays with cash. Brags he got the nickname from some sort of chain whip he uses."

My stomach turned as I connected the nickname with the flayed skin and clothing on two of the soldiers.

"Sick bastard," Michael said.

"Yeah, he's a real piece of work," Tom said. "Short guy... about five foot five, maybe a hundred and fifty pounds, but built like he spends a few days a week in the gym. Brown hair, droopy eyes, usually wears a suit, but I've seen him in jeans a time or two. Hits on all the girls but never leaves with one. Sometimes he comes in with a couple friends. I wish I had more to tell you. I'd like to see this low-life come to an abrupt end, if you know what I'm sayin'. I've got plenty of patrons warmin' my bar stools, and I don't need him bringin' trouble into the establishment."

"Thank you," Michael said, trying to give him a hundred-dollar bill, but Tom shook his head and pushed off the desk.

"If you guys can keep Chains from bringin' his sorry ass back here, that'd be thanks enough," he said, showing us out the back door.

Now that we had a name and a description, Chains wouldn't be too difficult to find, but it was almost six a.m. by the time we left the bar.

Michael drove to my parents' house to let the old man know what we'd found out and see what he wanted us to do from there while I tried to get a little shut-eye in the passenger's seat, but couldn't. The images of those two flayed men kept playing in my head. We needed to find this Chains son-of-a-bitch and make sure he never used that weapon again.

CHAPTER FOUR
Dominico

MY FAMILY OWNED two and a half acres outside of Vegas. Surrounded by eight-foot-high security fencing, the property kept guards posted around the clock. In addition to the main house, there were two in-laws' quarters. Michael and I lived in one of them, and off-duty family soldiers, who had been personally vetted by my father, slept in the other.

The traditional stucco buildings—combined with the swimming pool, armed soldiers, and high fences—made the estate look like some sort of Spanish villa for the cartel. Guards waved us through the gate, and Michael and I went straight to the main house where Mamma greeted us at the door, fussing about how tired we looked.

"Look at those bags under your eyes," she said, kissing Michael's cheeks. "I read an article the other day about missing sleep. They say it takes years off your life. You're both still growing, so you need your rest."

Mamma wasn't stupid. Her father had been the Mariani family boss, who—without any sons—had made her husband his heir. Mamma grew up as a *Dona*, the female equivalent of a Don, and she knew who we were, what we did, and that the chances of old age taking us to the grave were slim to none. Yet she still insisted on making sure we regularly ate well-balanced meals and nagged us about annual doctor and dentist visits like we were normal kids. We humored her whenever we could. After all, the fires of hell are nothing compared to the nagging of an Italian mamma.

"We're fine, Mamma," Michael assured her. "And you better hope Dom's done growing, or he'll have to duck to get in the doorways." My big brother had been sore about my height since I outgrew him right after my sixteenth birthday.

"Don't listen to him, Dom," she said, tugging on my suit until I bent down so she could give me a kiss. "You grow all you want. You're perfect. Both my boys are. Now go see your father, and I'll make you breakfast."

I wasn't hungry, but if Mamma had it in her mind to feed someone, you'd better believe they were gonna get fed, and no arguments could dissuade her. She scurried off toward the kitchen to do her thing while we headed to Father's office.

My old man's office was located on the main floor in the back of the house, overlooking the swimming pool. The room held a permanent fragrance of pine, gun oil, cigar smoke, and whichever monthly plug-in air freshener Mamma used to try to mask the odors. This month's vanilla scent hit us before we even opened the door. Leaned back in his desk chair, fast asleep, Father startled awake when the door creaked open. He had his hand on his gun before we crossed the threshold.

"Father," Michael said by way of greeting, easing into the room.

Looking from Michael to me, the old man released his Glock, lying it on the top of his desk. "Come in, boys. Sit."

The assortment of office furniture could comfortably seat eight. Sometimes Father held family meetings here, squishing us all together and making the soldiers stand in the back while those of higher rank sat in front. Pleasing the old man meant you got a seat, but if you pissed him off, you could be standing for years while fighting to get back in his good graces. It was his version of public humiliation and was surprisingly effective. None of the bosses liked to stand.

"I trust you have news," Father said, once we sat. His exact orders had been, "Don't come home until you know something," and neither Michael nor I would have been stupid enough to disobey that command.

Michael relayed the tale from the bartender while I gnawed on the inside of my cheek, trying to stay awake. Despite my best efforts my eyes must have drifted closed, because the next thing I knew, Michael's elbow was digging into my side. My eyes sprang open to find my father glaring at me.

"Shall I have your mamma bring you your blankie and teddy bear?" he asked.

I'd been awake for almost twenty-four hours, and sitting in his too-damn-comfortable office chair had finally done me in, but Father wasn't the type to accept excuses. I bolted upright and apologized.

"Stand," he said. "And try to stay awake."

I rose and stood behind my chair, careful not to touch it so he wouldn't accuse me of slacking. They continued their conversation while I stood guard like a sentry or a common soldier, exactly how the old man wanted me to feel. He and Michael spoke of plans involving me like I wasn't even in the room. Father would allow us a few hours of sleep, but he wanted us back on Chains's trail as soon as possible to track down his entire crew and bring them in for questioning.

The families kept the peace in Vegas... mostly. Only peace looked a lot like a shaky house of cards with a grenade on top. We knew the Durante family was behind the attack, and we sure as hell planned to retaliate. But if we could prove their involvement, their allies would be a little more hesitant to jump in and collapse the peace completely.

As the meeting's last order of business, Father gave me a task. "The new chef... make sure she gets to and from work every day. Keep an eye on her and let me know if the Durantes are sniffing around."

Babysitting a cook was the type of task he'd normally assign to a common soldier, and now he gave it to me as punishment. The rest of the crew would get a kick out of this for sure, but I couldn't force myself to get too upset about the chance to watch Annetta Porro's fine ass. Oh, I'd keep an eye on her all right. Trying not to sound too eager, I said, "Yessir."

"Did you find out what happened to the last chef?" Michael asked.

Father's eyes hardened. "One of Carlo's men found him back at his mom's house in Reno. Said someone threatened him into leaving town for a while."

The *chooch*, the moron, had run, and, judging by Father's reaction, the chef's temporary vacation had turned into a permanent one. The old man had no use for cowards or traitors. And if the Durantes had scared the old chef off, who knew what they'd do to the new one? Had I put Annetta Porro's life in danger by pushing for her to get the job?

By the time Father released us, worry and exhaustion left no room in my brain to even think about food. Mamma wouldn't hear of it, though. She sat both Michael and me down, plopping a giant slice of baked frittata in front of each of us. My sister, Abriana, wandered into the kitchen, poured herself a glass of orange juice, sat at the table, and stared out the window.

I nudged her under the table with my foot. "You okay, Bri?" I asked.

She shrugged. "Peachy."

Finishing up the dishes, Mamma paused long enough to frown at Abriana before tossing her towel on the counter and leaving. The instant she slipped out of sight, Abriana carried her glass of juice to the liquor cabinet and topped it off with vodka.

"Bri!" Michael reprimanded. "What the hell do you think you're doing?"

Our nineteen-year-old little sister shouldn't be partaking at all, but especially not at seven in the morning.

Abriana screwed the lid back on the vodka and set it in the cabinet. "Take a chill pill, Mikey. If I'm old enough for them to sell me off like some prized cow, I should be old enough for the hard stuff."

"A prized cow?" Michael snorted. "Someone's got a high opinion of herself."

She tilted back the glass, downing every drop before setting it on the counter. "Screw you."

"Poor little Abriana," he taunted. "You think it's any different for us? Do you honestly believe you're the only one Father's working on a marriage contract for?"

She blinked, looking to me for answers. I knew nothing, so I said, "You wanna fill us in, Mike?"

"You're twenty-three, Dom. I'm twenty-five. Only reason we're still single is that Father didn't want to tip his hand too soon. Now he's cementing his alliances and it's only a matter of time."

I don't know why I was shocked. There weren't many decisions that the old man let us make for ourselves, but for some reason I'd expected to be able to select my own wife. I felt sucker-punched as I stared at my brother, wondering how long he'd known about this. "Who's he hooking you up with?" I asked.

"One of the Caruso girls. I'm supposed to get to know them during Abriana's engagement dinner and tell him which one." Michael put his elbows on the table and cradled his head in his hands, staring at his plate.

My brother had secrets... secrets he was keeping from me.

I didn't want to know, but I refused to be a coward and forced myself to ask the question. "What about me?"

Michael looked at me and shrugged.

The bastard knew. I could see it in his eyes. "Don't you fuckin' lie to me, Mike. Who's he plannin' to saddle me with?"

"He told me not to tell you until the dance, but I think it's better that you have some time to come to grips with it." Michael took a drink and set down his cup.

That sounded bad. Not only was he stalling, but my brother had argued with Father about when to tell me? "Who the fuck is it?" I asked.

"Ciro Pelino's daughter. They'll announce it right after I get hitched."

Don Pelino only had one daughter. My memory served her up as being younger and quiet with a long face. The broad was supposed to be my bride and I couldn't even remember her name. I looked to Abriana for help.

"Valentina," she provided.

Michael nodded. "Don Pelino and Father have already started negotiating."

My world tilted on its axis. Throughout my entire life, Father had pointed out my shortcomings and uselessness. As the heir apparent, Michael was the one destined for a political marriage. Abriana would have probably gotten off the hook if she hadn't caught the eye of the son of Father's biggest California ally. As for me... I didn't need to produce an heir, so I'd been planning to stay single like Uncle Carlo. And if I couldn't stay single, I at least wanted to pick out the goddamn woman I had to marry.

"I hate this family," Abriana said. She pushed off the counter and headed outside.

"But we *love* you," Michael said mockingly.

"Don't be such a dick," I said to him before following my sister out to the back patio. She slunk down on a wicker sofa overlooking the pool, and I sat beside her. The orange glow of the rising sun reflected off the water as the air chilled my skin. I draped an arm over my sister and hugged her to my side.

She sighed. "What if he's a complete asshole?"

I rubbed her shoulder. "Mike? He's an asshole all right."

She elbowed me in the ribs. "You know who I'm talking about, Dom."

"I know." Although I felt bad for my sister, focusing on her problem while running on fumes and still trying to get over the shock of Michael's revelation about my own fate, proved difficult. "Sorry, sis, I'm still trying to digest this whole Valentina Pelino thing. Is she even an adult yet?"

Abriana shook her head. "No. She's a few years younger than me."

Disturbing. But at least that meant I had time.

"They'll probably let you two wait until she's eighteen," Abriana added, her mind obviously coming to the same conclusion. "Lucky."

"Lucky?" I asked. "Bri, that girl is boring. Have you ever tried to talk to her? She just giggles. And her face…"

Abriana sat up. "What's wrong with her face?"

"It's like a horse."

A bubble of laughter escaped from my sister's mouth before she suppressed it and shook her head at me. "You're awful, Dom."

I wasn't trying to be awful, I was being honest. "I'm not even kidding. Have you seen the size of that overbite? It'd be like going to bed with Mr. Ed."

She fought off another giggle. "Dom!"

"I know. That poor girrrrl," I whinnied.

This time, Abriana did allow herself to laugh. When her laughter died down, silence fell between us. She propped her head on my shoulder and we watched the sunrise together as my eyelids grew heavy.

After a while she said, "I know you and Mike will have to marry whoever Father selects too, but it's different for you."

I yawned. "Different how?"

She leaned away and pulled her feet up to the seat cushion. "Because you're men. If you don't like your wife, you can ignore her and take a mistress or two. Like Father."

Mobsters weren't exactly known for their monogamous relationships. I couldn't have been more than ten when Uncle Carlo and I were making a delivery and I saw Father's *consigliere*—his counselor—Giuliano Biondo, out to dinner with a woman on his lap. Assuming the woman was Giuliano's wife Celia—a kind woman who always gave me cookies when we stopped by her bakery—I rushed to their table to say hello. Carlo intercepted me, but not before I saw the woman's face... it wasn't Celia.

"Why would he cheat on Celia?" I asked Carlo as we left the restaurant.

"Mobsters take mistresses," he replied, brushing off the question.

"Why?"

"Lots of reasons. It's not like we live forever, kid. Those who don't get popped get pinched and end up doing hard time up the river. It's a rough life we lead, and we take pleasure wherever we can get it."

I studied him, absorbing everything he said. "Why aren't you married?"

He chuckled. "I don't need the liability."

"What does that mean?"

He shrugged. "We're surrounded by volatile men who will always try to get one up on you, but if you don't love anyone, they can't use anyone to get to you."

The memory made me wonder what sort of future my sister would have. Would Romario De Lucca love her and turn her into a liability one of his enemies could capitalize on? Or would she be home mothering his children while he spread his seed all over town like most of the mobsters I knew? They say you never really know how many kids a mobster has until his funeral.

But, since none of my musings would cheer Abriana up, I decided to lie through my teeth. "Father doesn't have a mistress."

She gave me a sideways you're-full-of-shit-and-we-both-know-it look. "You're right, he doesn't have a mistress. He has several... a fuckin' harem. You know the old man doesn't like to get attached. I don't know what they see in him, either. Mamma can barely stomach him, and she has to."

I put a finger to my lips and reminded my sister to keep her voice down. We'd both be in danger if Father or any guards looking for favor overheard us. "Money can be a powerful aphrodisiac," I whispered.

Abriana rolled her eyes. "Not that powerful. Goddamn pulsating cockstorm sperm lord."

I loved Abriana, but at nineteen, she'd never had to work a day in her life and had grown up behind the protection of Father's soldiers. A spoiled brat, but also a good girl—learning creative swear words had been the extent of her teenage rebellion—I had no idea how she'd make it as a mobster's wife. Nor had I ever heard anyone use the term "cockstorm" before. I had to give her points for her creativity.

"You're not thinking of taking a… a mister, are you?" I asked, trying to lighten the tone and keep her from running her mouth some more and getting us both in trouble.

"A mister?" She choked out a laugh. "Like a male mistress? As nice as that sounds, I'm not suicidal, Dom. The family doesn't care about any of this women's rights shit. Our dear ol' daddy already pulled me into his office to grill me and make sure I'm still a virgin and won't shame our family on my wedding night. Like any man would touch me, knowing who Father is. He gave me a full-on lecture about my duties as a wife… and oh, I'm well aware of the consequences if I dishonor him. We both know that even if Romario De Lucca beats the shit out of me, there won't be a soul on the planet who can help me."

"Bri—"

"I'm serious, Dom. You know I'm right. He could be a drunk who rapes me every night before visiting his whores, and who will care? Will Father? Will you and Mike swoop in and rescue me?"

"I—"

"No, you won't. You can't. Father needs the support of the De Luccas, and he would sacrifice every single one of us to get it. You know it, I know it, Michael knows it. Even

Mamma knows it. But none of us can do a damn thing about it, because it's what's best for the family." She spat. "Again, I hate this family."

"Don't talk like that, Bri. Especially not here. You know Father will flip out if he hears you."

"So? What can he do now?" She snorted. "For the first time in my life I'm actually valuable to him. He's not gonna hit me this close to the dinner. God forbid his allies find out what a monster he is."

"He's in a difficult position," I defended.

"I wonder if you'd be so understanding if he was ruining your life." She squeezed her knees to her chest.

I didn't know what more to say to my hurting little sister, so I gave her a hug and said what I could. "I'm sorry, Bri."

She wriggled out from under my arm and stood. "Yeah, me too." Then she headed back into the house.

CHAPTER FIVE
Annetta

I GOT THE *job!*
Even as I exited the bus to head in for my first day of work, I still couldn't believe it. The shock kept going as I tied on my apron and scrubbed my hands. Afraid Frank would be the one training me, I was pleasantly surprised when Brandon greeted me and led me to my station.

"I'll be working with you today," he said. "If you don't remember where everything is from your crash-course interview, just ask."

"Are you my boss?" I asked.

He chuckled. "Hardly."

"Is Frank?"

"No. You, Frank, and I all three answer directly to Collin." Then with a warm, genuine smile and a patient tone, he introduced me to the rest of the staff and spent the next couple hours walking me through the menu and policies and procedures.

Still excited and desperate to wring every drop of knowledge I could from him, I fired off questions and took detailed notes to study later. A couple of the other chefs gave me sideways glances, but I didn't care if my bubbly enthusiasm and giant notepad revealed my rookie status. It would all be worth it when I jumped right into the flow and blew away the kitchen's learning curve.

"We have a really important dinner coming up with about a hundred guests, so we're going to focus on getting you trained to whip out dishes in a high-stress environment. Normally training wouldn't be this intense, but after the last chef disappeared..." Brandon clamped his mouth shut.

"Disappeared?" I asked.

"I mean bailed," he amended, fidgeting with his apron. "Didn't even bother to give notice or call in and tell us he was done. Didn't even pick up his final check." His gaze went to a clipboard beside the grill. "Have I shown you this cleaning schedule yet?"

I let the abrupt topic change slide and shook my head, wondering what had really happened to the last chef. But I didn't have much time to think about it, because the restaurant got busy the moment the doors opened, and the workday raced by in a blur of orders. Both Frank and Collin made a few appearances, no doubt sniffing around to make sure I hadn't burned anything up or poisoned anyone, but for the most part everyone left us alone to work.

By the time I clocked out, my feet were aching, and I smelled like garlic and fish. I washed off as much of the funk as I could and let myself out the back door, stepping into a cloud of cigarette smoke. Waving my hand to disperse it, I headed for the bus stop.

"Annetta, wait," someone said.

I turned to find Dominico from the interview walking toward me, lit cigarette in hand. He had to be close to six-and-a-half feet tall, and the top of my head barely reached his shoulders. Clean-shaven with his dark hair combed back, he looked slick in his tailored suit. My gaze lingered on his broad shoulders and big arms for a moment longer than I'd intended. I couldn't help it. Although he was a pig, the man *was* hot. The kind of hot that made good girls make very bad decisions. He took one last drag before tossing the butt on the sidewalk and snuffing it out with a shiny black oxford.

The city buzzed around us, but the sidewalk where we stood seemed strangely isolated, making me feel vulnerable and exposed. Something dark and exciting danced in Dominico's bloodshot eyes, making me question the safety of being alone with him. Still, he had been in on my interview, so I needed to play nice.

"Can I help you?" I asked.

"Just thought I'd be friendly and walk you to your car," he replied.

Since it was none of his business that I couldn't afford a car, I said, "Thanks, but I can manage." I turned and continued toward the bus stop.

I heard the sound of his footsteps behind me, but kept going.

"But the parking lot's that way," he said.

Glancing over my shoulder, I confirmed that he was pointing the opposite direction and kept walking. "Neat."

"Don't you wanna go that way?" he asked.

Seeing no way to avoid telling him the truth, I said, "I'm riding the bus."

He hurried to get in front of me. "Will you just hold up a second?"

I stopped and put my hands on my hips, fully aware my stance would come off as hostile. I felt hostile. My feet hurt, my arms and shoulders felt like they were made of rubber, and I wanted to get home and relax. "Do you need something?"

He ran a hand through his hair, mussing it up. "Look, I'm sorry about yesterday. I wasn't feeling well, and realize I came off as sort of a dick."

His blunt self-examination surprised me, but I wasn't about to let him off the hook. "You were hungover and acting like a chauvinistic pig," I corrected.

One of his eyebrows shot up. He stared at me for a moment before shaking his head. "You sure don't pull your punches, do you?"

"Should I?" I asked. "A big boy like you should be able to take them."

Why did that sound like I was hitting on him? Appalled, I hurried to correct myself. "I mean... That didn't come out right."

He chuckled, his eyes sparkling with humor. "You sure?"

Gah, the man was infuriating. I tried to step around him, but he held out an arm, stopping me.

"You're right though, I did act like a chauvinistic pig... and a dick. Let me make up for it by giving you a ride home."

His apology seemed sincere, and I could tell he had a decent sense of humor, but I didn't know him from Adam. I'd heard plenty of stories about girls who got into cars with sexy men they didn't know and had no desire to become a statistic.

"Thanks, but no thanks. I'm good." But since I didn't want to be rude, I added, "See you tomorrow."

"What do you mean you're good? You don't have a car. You ride the bus. Let me take you home and save you some money."

"I like riding the bus." I did, too. It gave me a chance to unwind, and I liked people-watching. "And not that it's any of your business, but I can afford the fare."

He sighed, the corner of his mouth turning up in the sexiest smirk I'd ever seen. Butterflies danced in my stomach at the sight, and I struggled to remember why his remarks during the interview had seemed so insulting. Maybe my nerves had made me overly-sensitive.

"Sorry, I'm handling this all wrong," he said. "I'm in charge of security for the restaurant, and the manager asked me to make sure you got home okay. There's been some crime in the area lately, and he's a pretty old-fashioned guy."

"Collin sent you to offer me a ride?" I asked.

"Collin, yeah, that's the manager," Dominico replied.

The few brief times I'd seen him, Collin hadn't seemed overly concerned with my safety, but with Brandon's comment about my predecessor disappearing... I couldn't help but wonder if there was more to the story. "Is this about the chef who bailed?" I asked.

Dominico's eyes narrowed. "Who told you about that?"

Not wanting to sell Brandon out, I shrugged. "I can't remember. Maybe I heard about it on the news or read about it in the paper. I didn't realize he worked at this restaurant, though. Did he ever pick up his check?"

The way Dominico watched me made me feel a little uncomfortable. "Do you know him?" he asked.

"No."

"We haven't heard from him." He rolled his shoulders, not looking me in the eye. "We don't think it's connected to the restaurant—the guy had a gambling problem and probably split to get out of paying—but just in case, I'd like to take you home."

"So he *did* disappear. I thought he just quit."

Dominico snapped his mouth shut and shook his head. "Look, I'm trying to make sure you get home safe. Are you gonna let me give you a lift or not?"

I glanced down the street in time to see the bus pulling away from the stop, which meant I'd have to wait twenty minutes for the next one. I didn't know if my aching muscles could handle five.

"We can go in and Collin can vouch for me," Dominico offered.

I couldn't decide if it would make me feel more comfortable or like a paranoid idiot. After all, he'd been in on the hiring process and therefore clearly worked for the restaurant. He did seem legitimately concerned for my safety, and there was a fine line between independence and recklessness. I couldn't shake the feeling that there was more to my predecessor's disappearance than he was letting on.

"You promise you're not some sort of psycho killer or rapist or something?" I asked.

His sexy smirk widened into a full-fledged toothy smile as he held up his hand. "Scout's honor."

Nothing about him said Boy Scout, but I let the pledge slide and accepted the ride home. He led me to a sweet-looking black Porsche convertible and opened the passenger's side door.

"*This* is your car?" I asked.

He nodded. "Like it?"

Of course I liked it; it was sleek and shiny with tinted windows and what I'm sure were custom rims. Who wouldn't like it? "I love it, but I thought you said you worked security. How'd you end up with a car like this?"

He cocked an eyebrow at me and as I replayed the question in my head heat crept into my cheeks.

"Sorry, that was rude and it's none of my business. I suffer from a broken filter and have yet to learn what I should and shouldn't say out loud."

He gestured me into the car and shut the door before hurrying to the driver's side. The car's interior was even swankier than the outside. I snuggled into the leather seat and checked out the dashboard full of gauges.

"I like it," he said when he climbed in.

"The car? Me too. It's gorgeous. I've never ridden in a ragtop before." I studied the roof, wondering how it worked.

"No. Well, yes, but that's not what I was talking about. I like that you speak your mind. People don't usually do that around me. It's refreshing."

"Why? You some sort of royalty or something?"

"Not exactly, but my family is well off." He tapped the steering wheel a couple times, and then turned to face me. "Want me to put the top down?"

The chilly March air made me hesitate only a second. "Will you please?"

"Sure. You got a jacket?"

I nodded and tugged it out of the backpack at my feet. He beamed me another smile before flicking a switch on the dashboard. The top slowly receded, and I put on my coat and buckled my seat belt. Dominico turned the heater on our feet.

"What kind of music are you into?" he asked, fiddling with the radio.

"I'm good with whatever," I said, waving him off.

He cocked his head and looked at me. "But what do you like?"

For someone just trying to give me a ride, he sure asked a lot of questions. I couldn't help but be flattered by his interest. I'd always been a private person, though, so it felt weird to talk about myself.

"I promise not to use the information against you," he prodded.

"Oldies," I confessed.

"Oldies?" he asked. "What era are we talking here?"

"All of them, but mostly sixties."

"That's… unusual. I don't think I've ever met a girl under fifty who likes oldies. Is there a story behind it?"

I shrugged, not yet ready to reveal all my secrets. "Papa says I have an old soul."

He took his hand off the radio dial to shift into reverse. "Well, you're gonna have to help me out here, because I have no idea which radio stations play oldies."

"We don't have to listen to my music. You're already giving me a ride and I'm pretty sure that's above and beyond security guard duties. I'm good with modern stuff too."

"No way, now you've got me interested. I want to hear the kind of music a girl like you listens to." He backed out of the parking spot and drove toward the exit. "Change the station and tell me where I'm headed."

A girl like me?

I chewed on that while rattling off directions to my house and messing with the radio. It landed on Gladys Knight and the Pips' song "Midnight Train to Georgia," the very song my parents had been listening to when Mamma realized she loved Papa. I knew, because she must have told me the story a hundred times.

Hearing the song now, with Dominico, caused goosebumps to rise across my flesh. Which, in turn, made me feel stupid. Sure, he was being nice and giving me a ride home, but I barely knew the guy. I chalked the warm feelings up to watching too many romance movies with my sappy best friend.

"I like it," Dominico said, tapping his hand to the beat against the steering wheel.

I nodded. "It was my mom's favorite song."

"She had good taste," he replied. I appreciated the way he didn't ask about her and just let the topic drop. "You hungry? Want to stop somewhere and get something to eat before I drop you off?"

Driving me home because his boss asked him to was one thing, but he'd put down the top of his car in cold weather for me, let me choose the music, and now he wanted to feed me? My personal experience with guys was limited, but I'd heard enough stories to find his behavior unusual.

"Why are you being so nice?" I asked.

He eyed me, frowning. "I'm just… It's just… Are you hungry or not?"

And why did he sound so pissed? "I'm sorry, I didn't mean to upset you. Thank you for the offer, but I'm fine." I sniffed my clothes. "And in desperate need of a shower. Please just take me home."

We rode the rest of the way in silence, and when he pulled up in front of my house, he killed the engine, got out, and joined me on the curb.

"What are you doing?" I asked.

"Walking you to the door," he replied, gesturing for me to accompany him.

Confused, I asked, "Why?" It's not like we were on a date or something.

"Because it's dark and it's the right thing to do."

I pondered his answer as he led me to the door.

"What time do you work tomorrow?" he asked.

"Two. They're having me close. Why?"

"I'll be here at one thirty to pick you up."

I stopped. "You don't have to do that. I can take the bus."

"I do have to. My boss asked me to, remember?"

His answer reminded me our ride was just part of his job, which upset me for some strange reason. I don't know what I'd been expecting, but the disappointment stung. "Oh, yeah. Fine. I'll see you tomorrow."

I reached for the doorknob, but he got to it first, his hand freezing midturn. "Does that piss you off?" he asked, humor sparkling in his eyes as he watched me.

"No. I don't know. It shouldn't." I really wanted to get past him and into the comfort of my house.

His lips twitched like he was fighting off a smile, which actually did piss me off. "I'll see you tomorrow," he said, opening the door for me.

"Whatever," I said, stepping past him and into the house, where I caught Papa peeking through the blinds.

When the door closed behind me, he asked, "Who brought you home?"

I rolled my eyes. "He's nobody, Papa. Just one of the security guys from work."

Papa's eyebrows rose. "Nice car. They must pay their security well."

"Yeah." Too confused about Dominico to discuss him, I waved Papa off. "But don't you want to hear about my first day?"

He smiled and stepped away from the window to hug me. "Of course, luce dei miei occhi. How did it go?"

Thankful for his willingness to let all talk of that frustrating security guard drop, I gave him a full rundown on my day while I made us a snack, shoving Dominico and his flashy car firmly from my thoughts.

CHAPTER SIX
Dominico

*A*FTER I DROPPED Annetta's sweet ass off at her house, I headed to the casino for a meeting with Carlo. Taking my seat beside Michael, I waited as a few more soldiers from Carlo's team filed in.

When Carlo entered, he brought us up to speed on the details of the attack. Then Michael stood and gave everyone a rundown on what we'd found out about Chains before Carlo took over again.

"If you're on a job, I want you to continue it," he said, leaning against his desk. "We need to keep money flowing in, but every single one of you needs to be on the lookout for this *stronzo*, this bastard, and I want to know the instant you get eyes on him. Also, we know he didn't act alone. We need to pull him in alive, so we can pinch him for information on the rest of his crew and make him rat out his employer. They won't get away with this. Not a goddamn one of 'em."

Carlo released the team, but told me and Michael to hang back. Once his office cleared, he sat us back down and reminded us of our duty.

"Regardless of who finds Chains and his gang, your father wants you two to handle this," he said. "He wants you to make this asshole squeal like a pig."

Michael nodded, his expression guarded. "I figured as much."

I had, too, unfortunately. Father had people—people who could pry the deepest hidden secrets from anyone—but he insisted that me and Michael needed the experience, so lately we'd been getting all the torture gigs. Lucky us.

"I'm hoping we find them before this weekend, but if not, we're gonna need extra security at the engagement dinner. Since we don't want to look like we don't have our shit together, the boss has been hesitant to bring Don De Lucca in on our situation, but I don't know how long he can hold off. If the De Luccas feel we hid the information from them..." Carlo shook his head.

"When's Father gonna make the call?" Michael asked.

"Tomorrow evening. Unless we have Chains and his crew by then."

Michael blew out a breath. "Twenty-four hours doesn't give us much of a window."

"Do we have any leads?" I asked.

"I've got a guy inside the Durante family. He's been snooping around and found out Chains has a girlfriend who works at the Plaza. I reached out to her. She's not much of a girlfriend. Couldn't give me much on him—didn't even know his real name—but I did manage to squeeze his address and phone number out of her."

A guy inside the Durante family? I wondered who would be crazy enough to take that gig. Focusing on that was easier than allowing myself to think about whatever Carlo had done to "squeeze" the information out of Chains's girl. We couldn't afford to be lenient, especially not when our own guys had been killed in cold blood. But other than dating an asshole, she probably hadn't done anything wrong.

"I have a team watching his apartment, one on the Plaza, and one on his girlfriend's place. If he shows his mug, we'll know."

Michael nodded. "Tom has my pager number and promised to reach out if Chains, or any of the assholes he hangs with, shows up in his bar again."

"So now what? Back to the streets?" I asked, stifling a yawn. I'd gotten maybe eight hours of sleep over the last forty-eight hours and the idea of spending the rest of the day in the car made me want to pass out on the spot.

"Yep," Carlo said, clapping me on the shoulder. "And keep your eyes open. I heard you're already on babysitting duty, and I'd hate to see my brother have to discipline you again, Dom."

Discipline... a nice way of putting it. Like labeling the scars littering my body as "training." Nobody would ever accuse my old man of sparing any rods or spoiling any children.

"Yessir," I replied.

Carlo gave us a few locations to check into and dismissed us. Michael drove as I rattled off the businesses on Carlo's list. Each of the *borgatas* (crime families) had a turf consisting of businesses owned, ran, or protected. My family offered protection to several local shops, but our best investment had come in 1986 when Father had gone in with a couple of his allies to start up a corporation. They currently owned three casinos—the Big Top, the Oasis, and the Round Table—with plans for two more to go in toward the end of 1993. Father's most influential Las Vegas ally, Don Caruso, ran the Big Top. My family operated out of the Oasis, and the Round Table—which had only been open for two years—was currently in the hands of Don Pelino, boring Valentina's father.

Father's enemy, the reigning *capo dei cappi* (or boss of bosses) of Las Vegas, Don Maurizio Durante, owned a controlling share of our rival corporation, which currently held six casinos: The Pelican, Nero's, Sammy's, The Columbian, Blackbeard's, and Jafar's. The Durante family operated out of Nero's and the Columbian, putting their allies in charge of the others. My family made nice with Don Durante's allies, but we stayed the hell out of any properties Maurizio ran directly. I wouldn't put it past the crazy son-of-a-bitch to gun us down in cold blood as soon as we walked through the door. Best not to tempt him.

Still, Carlo had kept all rival casinos off our list. Everyone knew Michael and I were Marianis, so we'd have cameras on us from the moment we entered the lobbies and nobody would dare talk to us. Instead, we stuck to neutral casinos, not owned or protected by either family.

We covered the Mojave, the Caribbean, and the Imperial Casino. In each, we respectfully approached the managers and explained enough to show Chains as a threat we needed to unite on, while careful not to make our family sound vulnerable or weakened by the attack. The managers promised to alert their staff and pass on the information about the reward being offered.

After the casinos, we started the onerous task of covering Vegas's many restaurants. On our fifth one, we stumbled across another lead.

"Yeah, I know Chains," a cook by the name of Leslie said.

We'd caught her out back of some greasy spoon restaurant off East Desert Inn Road, dingy apron slung over her shoulder as she puffed on a lit cigarette. I lit up my own smoke and joined her.

"What'd that idiot do now?" she asked.

Michael avoided her question by asking one of his own. "How do you know him?"

"Used to work with his mom. Nice lady, but she let that boy run over her from the day he was born. I told her she needed to put her foot down and kick his ass every now and again, but she had guilt about his daddy being wrapped up in some mob." Leslie paused long enough to eye me and Michael in our suits. "You're not with the one of the mob families, are you?"

"No ma'am," Michael said. He pulled his wallet out and flashed her a fake badge. Most of the time our family credentials busted down the doors we needed opened, but sometimes a badge worked better. Ours were barely higher quality than toys—fake enough looking that if we were ever caught, our attorney could make the argument that nobody would accept them as real—but people rarely looked closely enough to notice. "We're detectives with the Las Vegas PD. We believe Chains messed up and got himself involved in a robbery that went south. Two men are dead, and we need to find him and ask some questions."

"You're shittin' me," Leslie breathed out.

"No ma'am," Michael replied.

She blew out a stream of smoke before snuffing out her cigarette. "Damn, that's a shame. Can't say I'm surprised, though. I'm tellin' you, I tried to warn her about that boy."

Sensing Leslie wasn't the sharpest knife in the restaurant, I jumped in to move the conversation along. "We need to find him as soon as possible. Your friend probably doesn't know what her son did. But it'll hit the news tonight, and then if we find him staying with her, she'll be arrested for harboring a criminal. The DA will stack up as many charges on her as he can... obstructing justice, aiding and abetting, you name it."

"But she... she'd never do anything like that. Only thing you could charge her with is loving her son too damn much and not knowing when to say no."

"We know that," Michael said, raising his hands. "But we gotta get Chains locked up before the news airs and the DA can start making a case against her. Most likely one of her neighbors already knows if Chains is staying with her. The family of the deceased is offering a decent reward for information so..."

"Oh?" Leslie asked.

It took everything I had not to shake my head in disgust. Carlo always harped on the payout mentality of Vegas, insisting most everyone in the city believed they'd hit the jackpot someday. Which explained the city's love of lawyers and malpractice suits. Those who couldn't win big, sued big.

Learning how to hustle meant using that mentality against people, and judging by the gleam in Leslie's eyes, she saw her potential payout on the horizon. I'd been trying to win her over by manufacturing concern for her friend, when Leslie would have gladly blabbed the second I waved a few bills under her nose.

"Yes ma'am," Michael said. "Ten thousand for information leading to the arrest and conviction of Chains."

We could have offered a hundred thousand, because Chains would never be arrested or convicted. He needed to die horribly and swiftly, preferably after he ratted out his crew. Leslie didn't know that, though, and I could almost see the wheels spinning in her brain, going over ways she could spend the money. Forcing her mouth into a frown, she looked back to me.

"A reward like that and Glenda would turn him in herself," she reasoned, letting Chains's mom's name slip out.

"We're gonna need a last name too," Michael said.

"Rollins. Glenda Rollins. She lives in a little two-bedroom house on Heart Avenue, across the street from an auto shop."

"Chains's real name?" I asked.

She looked from me to Michael, and then whispered, "Arthur. Arthur Rollins."

Michael and I thanked her for her time, took down her name and phone number for the imaginary reward, and headed to Heart Avenue to check up on Glenda Rollins. It was almost nine p.m. by the time we parked in front of a small canary-yellow bungalow across the street from a graffiti-covered auto repair shop. A boarded up abandoned house was Glenda Rollins's closest neighbor. With the windows dark and no car in the driveway we figured nobody was home, but knocked anyway. No answer, so we left our pager numbers with the neighbors and headed for a payphone to check in with Carlo.

Carlo said he'd send in a team to keep watch over the house and told us to get back to hitting up the restaurants. I

dragged my tired ass back to Michael's car, and we continued our search.

CHAPTER SEVEN
Annetta

RUE TO HIS word, Dominico picked me up and took me to work the next day. When I finished my shift, he was once again leaning against the wall by the back door, waiting. It made me realize that other than during my interview I had yet to see him actually working in the restaurant. I'd asked a couple of the kitchen staff about him, but they all looked at me like I was crazy.

Brandon went so far as to insist we didn't have security and recommended I stay far away from anyone who pretended to hold the position. But Dominico *had* been present during my interview, had been a perfect gentleman while driving me to and from work, and I couldn't deny the little thrill I got from finding him waiting for me.

"Hey, how was work?" he asked, taking my backpack from me.

"Busy. Crazy. I think Collin's gonna blow a gasket over this dinner coming up." Then my brain kicked in and reminded me that Dominico and my boss were probably close, and that I should keep my big mouth shut. "I mean, I know it's gotta be stressful for him, and I don't mean to sound critical, I just wish he wasn't so..."

"Wound up?" Dominico provided.

I nodded. "Yeah. At least I finally got him to filter his freakouts through me, rather than going directly to the staff. It's helping me earn their respect."

"Wait, he yells at you?" he asked, his brow furrowing.

"And you want him to?"

I shrugged. "He growls, but doesn't bite. I can take it. And it's part of the job, you know? I signed up for this, and I'm glad he's trusting me to do my job. But enough about my drama, how was your day?" I took a good look at Dominico, noting his rumpled suit and bloodshot eyes. "I'm guessing... rough?"

"You could say that." He gestured me toward the parking lot and we started walking. "The boss is riding my ass about this dinner, too. I've got some things to take care of so I can focus on security. Lots to do, unfortunately."

"I hear ya."

He opened the car door for me and I slid in. When Dominico got behind the steering wheel, he turned to face me and said, "Right now I could go for a nice cold beer, though. You feel like grabbin' a drink?"

"I don't think that's a good idea."

"Why not?"

I sniffed my hair. "For one, I smell like I've been cooking for eight hours. For two, I'm still wearing my uniform."

"So? People will know you work. It's not a big deal." His voice took on a pleading tone. "Come on, Annetta. It sounds like you could use a beer as much as I can."

A drink did sound good. More than that, I kind of enjoyed Dominico's company and wanted to spend a little more time with him. My best friend had been out of town with her family on vacation for more than a week now, and I missed just hanging out with someone. Still, I resisted. "I'm not much of a beer person."

"Great. We'll go somewhere that serves everything. What do you like?"

"Fruity drinks, low on the alcohol."

"I know just the spot," he said, starting the car.

Dominico took us to a small bar not far from the restaurant. I felt super self-conscious about my work clothes and stench until we walked in and past a table of dusty construction workers. Apparently this was the watering hole for working-class locals. We sat in a tucked away corner booth and I sipped on a piña colada while he drank a beer.

"Tell me something about yourself," he said.

"Like what?" I asked.

"What's your family like?"

"Not much to tell. It's just me and Papa. He works at the paper mill. I cook. Our lives are positively riveting."

He chuckled. "What do you do for fun?"

Fun? Who had time for fun? "Read. Watch T.V. Accept rides from strangers."

Dominico nodded, pounded out a cigarette, put it up to his lips, and lit it. "Can I ask how your mom died?"

Talk about a mood killer. Disappointed that he'd steer the conversation in that direction, I looked away and replied, "Lung cancer."

"Shit. Sorry. Did she smoke?"

"Not once. She worked in a restaurant. The doctors said secondhand smoke did her in."

Dominico swore again and snuffed out his cigarette. "Sorry."

Everyone said they were sorry when they heard about my mom, but the unexpected sincerity in his voice warmed me. "It's okay." I eyed the pack of cigarettes. "It's not a big deal for most people. For me, it… it's complicated."

He nodded. "I get it. So, she worked in a restaurant? Was she a cook like you?"

"No. Mom got pregnant with me right out of high school. She and Papa eloped, moved out here from the east coast, and she took the first job she was offered and stayed there until she died."

Dominico watched me. "She worked... did what she had to do. No shame in that."

"Yeah, and she was happy. *We* were happy. Papa hated it, though. He wanted her to go to school and do something more with her life. I think he always felt guilt about... well, me." I shook my head, annoyed with myself for sharing so much. "Sorry. I'm not good at small talk. I know it's supposed to be surface information, but I like it when it goes deep."

My mouth snapped shut as I realized all the inappropriate ways that could be taken. What was it about this guy that made me blurt out inappropriate crap? My cheeks felt like they were about to burst into flames. "The conversation, that is," I hurried to say.

Dominico laughed. I'd been fidgeting with a napkin and he trapped my hands in his, sprouting goosebumps up my arms.

"I want you to feel comfortable telling me anything. Everything," he said. "We can go deep any time you want."

His voice was husky and his tone was suggestive. Something hungry and exciting lurked within his dark eyes, inviting me to come out and play. And I wanted to. It was a serious struggle not to crawl across the table and straddle him right there in the restaurant. What the hell was wrong with me? Looking away, I fought for control of my misbehaving libido.

"I want to get to know you, Annetta. How does your father feel about you working in the restaurant?"

I tugged my hands out from under his, instantly missing the contact. I needed something else to keep them busy, so I pulled my drink closer and played with the straw. "We're still arguing about it. He wants me to go back to school, but it's so dang expensive and we already owe enough. Besides, I enjoy being in the kitchen. Mom taught me how to cook and when I'm doing it, I feel like she's not really gone, you know? Like part of her still lives through what she taught me."

He nodded. "I get it."

Still, I felt lame. "Why am I doing all the talking? What about you? What's your family like?"

His pager went off. He excused himself and used the bar phone while I fished fruit out of my drink, hoping he wouldn't catch me dripping alcohol all over the table, but unable to resist the rum-soaked pineapple.

When Dominico returned, he seemed upset and distracted. "Work calls. Come on, I need to get you home." He tugged a few bills out of his wallet and dropped them on the table before leading me out the back door.

Once we were in the car, he thanked me for coming out with him and claimed he had a good time.

I did too, even though our night had been cut short. "You must not get out much," I replied. "I did nothing but talk about myself, and I'm pretty boring."

"Not at all. I work a lot and the people I usually hang out with are... different. Trust me, this was nice." He pulled out of the parking lot and then grabbed my hand. Warmth crept up my arm.

The drive to my house was quiet as I wondered what this was between us and where it was going. Were we dating? Good friends? When had he transitioned from the mysterious security guy I never saw at work to taking me out to a drink and holding my hand? I was no closer to answers when he walked me to my door and said a hurried goodbye before jogging back to his car. I waved goodbye and stepped into the house, strangely disappointed that he hadn't kissed me.

*   *   *

The rest of the week passed in a blur. Dominico picked me up and dropped me off after every shift. He was always polite—holding doors and making sure I got in okay—but something had changed between us. He didn't really look at me, didn't invite me out for another drink, and he seemed to go out of his way to avoid touching me. With each passing day he seemed more distracted and worried. I still hadn't seen him around the restaurant during my shift, so I had no clue what his duties included, but they were clearly weighing on him. By the time he picked me up for my closing shift Friday afternoon, he looked strung out.

"You okay?" I asked as he walked me to his car.

"Yeah." He raked a hand though his dark hair, looking up and down the street. Vigilant security guard, constantly watching for threats. "I just got a lot going on right now."

As we drew closer to the engagement dinner, everyone at the restaurant was on edge. Despite the many times I'd asked, nobody would give away the names of the couple who'd rented out the entire restaurant for a night. The last time I asked, Frank glared at me and Brandon pulled me aside and suggested I let it go. Which, of course, only made me want to know more. I'd gone so far as reading gossip magazines to see if I could figure out which couple the restaurant could be hosting. Maybe a movie star or a local celebrity? And why was everyone being so tight-lipped about it?

Dominico was security. Not only security, but probably some sort of management to be in on the interviews. He'd have to know who was coming. I climbed into his Porshe and buckled my seatbelt.

"Must be some high-profile couple to have everyone so worked up about their engagement dinner," I said, fishing for information as Dominico settled himself behind the wheel.

He frowned and started his car.

He wasn't going to answer me either. Frustrated, I said, "Oh come on, just tell me who it is already."

He still didn't answer.

"Fine. Don't tell me. I'll guess. Whitney Houston and Bobby Brown? I read that they're gonna tie the knot this year, and it would be so cool to cook for their party."

"It's not Whitney and Bobbie." His frown deepened. "Nobody that well-known. In fact, it's not nearly as big of a deal as everyone's making it out to be. You've never heard of the couple. If I told you who they were, you'd be disappointed."

Doubtful with all the hoopla going on. He had to be trying to pacify me. "Oh come on, give me a hint. Is it... a senator or something?"

"Nope."

"Then why all the secrecy?" I asked.

He shrugged. "The family of the bride has... enemies. They asked us to keep a lid on the party."

"Enemies?" I let the word sit between us for a moment, wondering what sort of family would have enemies. It had to be a politician, which *was* disappointing. A singer or an actor would have been much more exciting. Still, enemies... "Will we be in danger?"

"No." Dominico released the gear shift to squeeze my hand. It was the first time he'd touched me since the night we went out for drinks, and my stupid stomach fluttered at the contact. He looked at me, and something in his eyes softened. "Mike and I are very good at what we do. We won't let anyone hurt you."

I blinked, and his gaze drifted back to the road. He withdrew his hand to shift again, and I immediately missed his touch. He left his free hand on the gearshift and did not reach for me again. He'd been so distant lately. I opened my mouth to ask him why, and then snapped it shut. We'd gone out for a drink, but Dominico must have friend-zoned me. No biggie. We'd only known each other for a short time. Not like I'd fallen for the guy or anything. So why did my chest feel so tight? Confused and hurt, I stared out the window for the rest of the drive.

CHAPTER EIGHT
Annetta

"THERE IS NOTHING to tell," I said for the umpteenth time, rolling my eyes.

Adona Micheli, my best friend since first grade who was finally home from her family vacation, sat cross-legged on my bed, bugging me for details about my non-existent relationship with Dominico, while I got ready for work.

"There *is* something," she insisted. "You said he took you out for drinks... and then nothing? Come on! No good night kiss? No promise to see you again? Nothing?"

"I told you, it was friendly. We'd both had a rough day, and he took me out for a drink as a nice gesture. I've seen him since. He's still picking me up and dropping me off every day."

Her eyebrows crept up her forehead. "But you're saying he's not interested in you?"

After last night I was certain of it, unfortunately. "Not in the least." I plugged my curling iron into the socket and set it on top of my dresser. Adona's family was wealthy. She got to sit at a cute and functional well-lit vanity when she applied her makeup. I had a ratty old dresser with a mirror attached. I squinted and wished for better lighting as I brushed my lashes with mascara.

"I doubt it." She pulled a small round packet out of her purse and set it on my dresser. "And you need to start taking these pills just in case."

My best friend had been trying to give me birth control since we were sixteen. I'd never needed them before, and I was reasonably sure I still didn't. Done with makeup and on to hair, I squirted a palm-sized amount of mousse into my hand and turned to frown at her. "I said nothing's going on, Adona. Are you calling me a liar?"

"Nope. I'm calling you clueless."

"I'm not clueless," I argued, drenching my curls in foam, trying to control them.

"Yes you are. Case in point: Kyle Morris was crushing all over you throughout our entire senior year, and you had no idea."

"Kyle Morris took Savannah Thompson to prom. If he liked me half as much as you swear he did, why didn't he ask me?"

Adona threw her head back dramatically. "Because he asked you to go to lunch and you said no."

"I brought lunch that day. Why would I go out and spend money?" I asked. We'd had this argument more than a dozen times, and I still couldn't see why one lunch would determine whether or not a guy asked me to a dance.

"And that's what I'm talking about." She shook her head. "Clueless."

Clearly, I still didn't get it. "Okay, fine," I conceded. "So how do I know if Dominico likes me?" My chest squeezed at the thought. Stupid emotions. I stuffed them down deep and frowned at my reflection in the mirror.

"Easy. I'm sticking around until he picks you up," she said, drifting to my bedroom window which faced the street. "I'll watch you two interact and let you know. Now… what do you think he's like in bed?"

She could be so ridiculous sometimes. Here I was, trying to get ready for the night my boss had been freaking out about since he hired me—the night of the super important party—and my best friend wanted me to fantasize about going at it with a guy who'd taken me out for a drink and basically ignored me since. Not like I hadn't imagined kissing his sexy lips and running my hands down his firm body, but sex? My cheeks warmed just thinking about it.

"He's just being nice. That's it."

She sighed. "I wish you'd embellish a little. You know my love life is DOA, and I'm trying to live vicariously through you. Give me something."

"Dead on arrival?" I asked. "What happened to Danny?"

Adona went through two things faster than anyone I'd ever known: shoes (currently adorning her feet were the new stars and stripes Keds) and guys (her latest conquest being a football player from UNLV named Danny).

"Oh he was pretty," she sighed. "But I got tired of having to compete with the mirror for his attention."

I giggled. "You're awful."

"I'm serious! You've never tried to have a conversation with him. If there's a reflective surface nearby, forget about it. He's checking his hair and his teeth and not paying attention to anything I say. Why can't I find a rich hottie who dotes on me like a queen? Then I can drop college and parade around in my bikini twenty-four-seven, providing him with eye candy like my stepmom does for my dad. Is that too much to ask? Speaking of which... hello, hot stuff. Please tell me this hunk in a three-piece-suit is not your boy toy."

I looked over her shoulder to see a dark-haired guy getting out of a blue BMW. Too short to be Dominico, but I recognized him immediately. "Nope. That's Mario. He was one of the guys who interviewed me, but I haven't seen him since. Wonder why he's here."

"Who cares?" Adona headed for the mirror above my dresser, pulling her sweater off her shoulder and wiping away makeup smudges under her eyes. "More importantly, is he single?"

My doorbell rang and Adona and I hurried to answer it. She beat me to the handle and flung it open before leaning against the door frame.

"Hello," she said, her voice breathy from sprinting.

"Hi." His brow furrowed, and his gaze went over her shoulder to find me. "Hey, Annetta. Dom's busy with the party and couldn't get away to pick you up this morning, so he asked me to."

Adona's gaze pleaded with me to make introductions, so I did. Mario shook her hand, and the smile she gave him was suggestive and a little frightening. Based on his amused smirk, I don't think he minded, though. Where Dominico was dark and mysterious, Mario had a cute and charming Peter Pan look about him.

"Very nice to meet you," Adona said. Then to me she added, "And make sure you take those damn pills."

She slipped Mario a piece of paper that I'm pretty sure had her phone number on it before he and I climbed into his Bimmer and motored off.

"Sorry about that," I said.

He chuckled. "No problem. She seems... fun."

Worried he'd say something like crazy or horny, I was relieved he'd settled on fun, and nodded in agreement. "Yep. Never a dull moment around that one."

His grin only widened. "I could work with that."

Thankfully Mario didn't expand on how, but I had a sneaking suspicion he'd be giving Adona a call. We spent the rest of the drive chatting about the restaurant, and by the time he parked I felt like I'd made a new friend. I thanked him for the ride and slipped in through the back entrance.

The flurry of kitchen activity tensed my shoulders immediately. Determined to stay cool and collected, I rolled them back, washed up, and headed to my station. Three dishes were on the menu for the dinner, one of which was the Linguine di Mare I'd made during my interview. I'd be taking point on that dish, so I got to work prepping it for the approximate number of guests Collin and I had estimated would order it.

After my prep work was done, I helped one of the other chefs. I didn't even get a break before the orders started rolling in, and the next several hours were spent boiling, sautéing, and chopping. My first break didn't come until well after we'd served dessert, and by then my bladder was about to burst. Since the employee restroom was occupied, I removed my apron and cap and headed for the customer bathroom.

Piano music played in the main room. I glanced inside long enough to confirm that the plates had been cleared away and several of the tables were pushed to the side to open up the dance floor. Men wore tuxes and the women sported fashionable gowns, each no doubt costing more than I made in a year. A lovely pink gown worn by a girl who I'd guess to be still in high school caught my eye. Plain-faced, with brown hair styled up on top of her head in a complicated-looking braid and heavy makeup, she looked like a little girl playing dress up.

She caught my eye because I recognized the smartly dressed, handsome man she was on the arm of.

Dominico returned her smile and patted her arm as he bent to say something.

He had a girl.

Wonder what that little wannabe tramp would think about him taking me out for a drink and holding my hand?

Ugly thoughts about something that was none of my business. Disgusted with myself and desperate to flee the scene, I tore my gaze away from them and hurried to the bathroom on autopilot. I'd known he was a player from day one and I was foolish to think he'd turn out being different, so why did my eyes burn and my chest hurt? I shoved through the doors and found an empty stall. There I leaned against the wall and tried to figure out why my heart felt like it had been ripped out of my chest and stomped on.

I was a reasonable person, and nothing about what I felt now was reasonable. It had to be Adona's fault for putting those ridiculous fantasies about Dominico in my head. I forced myself to take a couple of deep breaths and tried to let the ridiculous notion of me and Dominico being more than friends go. I clearly felt more for him than a friend should, so I needed to stop accepting rides. It wasn't fair to his girl-friend, after all.

And what did he see in that girl anyway? She was way too young for him. What sort of creep was he? And my god, her makeup! The trampy little bitch!

What is wrong with me?

I shook my head, appalled at my thoughts. Dominico *had* lied to me. Which would explain why my cheeks felt like they were on fire and I desperately wanted to punch something. He said he worked security, but he sure as heck didn't appear to be working tonight. No, he was definitely entertaining. Or being entertained. Why?

Maybe they're related?

Wishful thinking. I'd seen the way she looked at him. If she was family, then she had some sort of sick and twisted crush on her kin. But really, who could blame her? Certainly not me. I didn't even want a relationship, and Dominico's charm had done me in.

So you have a stupid crush. Get over it.

As I tried to talk my heart into not hurting, the bathroom door opened, and giggling voices drifted in.

"Ohmigod, he is so fine. I can't believe how lucky you are, Valentina," a voice said. "Your dad said it's for sure?"

"Yep," another girl replied.

Not wanting to be accused of eavesdropping on customers and losing my job, I flushed the toilet and headed out of the stall to wash my hands.

The girl in the pink dress had brought in an equally young-looking friend. "Michael has to get married first, because that's the way these things work," she said, applying even more makeup to her already overly-painted face. "But Don Mariani will announce Michael's engagement as soon as Abriana's on her honeymoon. Michael should be married by the time I turn eighteen."

Michael from my interview? Michael, Dom's brother?

"Michael is dreamy, too," the first girl said. She wore a peach chiffon dress and had gems in her hair and stars in her eyes. I kind of wanted to smack them both into reality. High school girls should be focusing on their futures and realizing their own dreams. Not fawning over some way-too-old for them boys. "I wonder who he's gonna marry?"

"Father said Michael will end up with one of the Caruso girls, but I don't know which one."

"Well one of those girls will end up very happy. Can you imagine being lucky enough to be married to the Mariani heir?"

"Hey, I'm not doing bad. I mean, Dom is a lot hotter than Michael." She sighed.

Married… to Dom. She'd said her dad had confirmed it. I felt sucker punched. Forcing myself not to react, I kept my gaze lowered, dried my hands, and headed out the door. The stupid, girly part of me wanted to rush out of the restaurant and hop on the first bus home, but thankfully the practical side kicked in, forcing me to march back into the kitchen and finish my job. I'd worked hard for this opportunity, and I sure wasn't going to let some stupid crush on some boy I barely knew ruin it.

"You okay?" Brandon asked the second he saw my face.

"Oh yeah, fine. Just tired." I forced a smile and batted away his concern with a hand. "Let's get this finished up so we can all go home."

I busted my butt to get out of there while my brain worked out the puzzle. Brandon had been right, Dominico didn't work there. The party must have been for someone in his family… a family so important he and Michael had been in on hiring the help for it. Dominico was dating the jail-bait in the pink dress, and eventually they'd get married. No big deal. It's not like we had anything going on. And good riddance! After all, I had no room in my life for some rich, smooth-talking charmer.

So why did my chest suddenly feel like a gaping hole?

Unable to reason my stupid emotions away, I focused on scrubbing my station until it sparkled. Then, because I didn't know who—if anyone—would be waiting for me outside the restaurant, I asked Brandon if I could bum a ride.

"Yeah, of course," he said, grabbing his keys out of the break room. "You want to grab a drink at that bar on the corner first?"

A drink? My chest hurt so bad I wanted to down the liquor of an entire bar to kill the pain.

I must have hesitated too long, because Brandon hurried to add, "Just as friends. To celebrate that this dinner is finally over, and things can get back to normal."

Now that was something I could drink to. I hoped to never see Dominico again.

Forcing a smile, I said, "I'm in."

Ten minutes later I sat on a barstool beside Brandon and ordered something fruity and loaded with alcohol. I downed it and nibbled on the pineapple slice while I ordered another, and another. In fact, I have no idea how many drinks I downed that night. Thankfully Brandon must have been a gentleman, because I vaguely recall him pouring me in and out of his car and helping me to my front door. Everything after that was a blur.

Turns out alcohol only made things worse, because the next day, my head hurt right along with my heart.

CHAPTER NINE
Dominico

FOR THE MOST part, the engagement party went off without a hitch, yet still managed to be a complete nightmare. Thanks to Annetta's culinary wizardry, the seafood pasta was great—I heard nothing but compliments about the other dishes as well—and all the bosses appeared to enjoy themselves. But being around Valentina gave me my first peek into my own personal Freddy Krueger-inspired nightmare to come. And judging by the forced smile stretched across Abriana's face, she felt trapped in the same horror flick.

I sidled up to my sister and asked, "Hey, how you holdin' up?"

"It's like I'm not even here," she replied, glaring daggers at her fiancé. "I think he's talked to everyone in the building *but* me. If this is any indication of what our marriage will be like, I'll need pets—lots of pets—to keep from talking to myself."

Mobster wives were often lonely, and Abriana and I had witnessed enough of Mamma's isolation to know how often

Father neglected her. Mamma never seemed to mind, though. She stayed busy with us, through volunteering with the PTA, and, in more recent years, by surrounding herself with other wives. In fact, Mamma seemed happier and more relaxed when my old man stayed out of the house. Whenever he was home the whole household tiptoed on eggshells, careful not to piss him off.

Since I didn't want to tell Abriana she might be better off not having the attention of her fiancé, I squeezed her shoulders and did my best to reassure her. "You'll get through it. We'll help you."

She frowned. "I know, Dom. It's just not what I expected."

Curious, I asked, "What did you expect?"

"Some sort of acknowledgment of my existence would be nice." She raised her chin and looked across the dance floor. "You have a borderline stalker on your hands. My God, Dom, she's just a kid."

I followed her gaze and suppressed a groan at the sight of Valentina Pelino smiling and waving at me. I'd never realized how young she was until that night. "I know! She keeps talking about her high school prom like she's waiting for me to ask her to it."

Laughter bubbled up from Abriana's chest. I glared at her.

"Better tell her you didn't even go to your own prom," she said.

School was never for me. I'd spent barely enough time at a desk to learn the necessities before Father yanked me out and put me to work. I could read orders, write a coded message, count money, and tell when someone was skimming off the top. What more did the second son of a mob boss need? I didn't even make it through tenth grade.

"Well, at least she's into you," Abriana said. "It's kinda sweet."

"Yeah. Sweet." I forced a smile and returned Valentina's wave, which unfortunately encouraged her to approach.

"You look beautiful, Abriana," Valentina gushed. "Congratulations on the engagement."

"Oh yes, I'm so lucky," Abriana replied, her sarcasm clearly lost on the girl, who giggled and batted her lashes before tugging me toward the dance floor like an overzealous puppy.

I didn't want to be rude and offend her or her family, but I'd mistaken Valentina for boring, never realizing how annoying she could be. I missed her boring side so damn much I wanted to shoot her just shut her up. I'd rather be chained to a corpse than babysitting some bubbly idiot. She blabbed on about high school drama while I bit my tongue and zoned out, nodding whenever she paused. She spoke of no goals beyond graduation, marriage, and children, and bragged about her old man like he was some sort of superhero who solved all her problems, rather than a crime lord who made people disappear.

I suffered through two chatter-filled dances before Mario slipped in through the side door and waved me and Michael over. Thankful for the interruption, I excused myself and followed my brother. We slipped out the side door to where Mario waited.

"What's up?" Michael asked, looking up and down the street. "Where's the crew?"

Since pretty much my entire family had been roped into entertaining, Mario was running security. We should have numerous men within sight, and I didn't see a one. Something must have happened. My back tensed, and I reached for my pistol. Michael already had his gun in hand.

"Busy, but don't worry." Mario glanced at the two nearest buildings. "Snipers still have eyes on this entrance and two more of our soldiers will be here soon. We caught some kid sniffin' around the cars. Got him detained in the storage room and thought you two might want to be there when we question him."

"Yes," Michael and I both said, sounding entirely too enthusiastic about the interruption to our evening. My brother's selection of a Caruso girl must have been going about as well as my time with Valentina.

We circled the building and Mario unlocked the back door, letting us in. We could still hear the music from the party in the front of the restaurant, but it was muted to a dull roar, which meant nobody up front would overhear our questioning. Good to know.

The storage room was about ten-feet by thirty-feet, and all four walls were lined with shelves full of supplies, leaving a small rectangle of empty space in the center. Currently crammed into that space were four soldiers surrounding a kid roped to a chair and gagged with a hand towel. The kid couldn't have been more than sixteen or seventeen, his clothes were baggy, his legs and arms were scrawny, and he was sporting one hell of a shiner. As I drew near, I couldn't help but notice his dilated pupils and runny nose.

"Has he said anything yet?" Michael asked as we squeezed into the small space with the others.

"Won't shut up," replied one of the soldiers. "Hopped up on coke and runnin' his mouth, but not a damn word of it was useful. We had to gag him to get some peace."

Michael nodded. "Go back to your assignments. We can handle it from here."

All four soldiers filed out of the room, and Mario closed the door behind them. Michael approached the kid's side, fisting his shaggy blond hair to pull his hair and force him to look up. The kid grunted around the gag.

"Do you know who I am?" Michael asked.

The kid shook his head.

Michael roughly tugged the kid's head down to see me and Mario. "What about them? You know who they are?"

The kid shook his head again.

"Here's what's gonna happen," Michael said, pulling the kid's face back up to look at him. "I need you to focus. I'm gonna take this gag off and ask you some questions. You answer them truthfully, you walk out of here alive. You lie to me, I'm gonna break every bone in your body. Slowly. You get me?"

Eyes wide, the boy nodded.

Michael didn't even bother untying the gag. He whipped out the switchblade strapped to his ankle, stared the boy down, and he sliced through the towel. The boy was trembling by the time Michael asked the first question.

"Who hired you?"

"N-n-nobody," the kid stammered. "I was just lookin' for a car to steal. I have this friend who wants a nice Lam and I saw one out there and thought I could nab it and make some money for my mom because she's sick and—"

"Shhh," Michael said, pressing the flat end of his switchblade to the boy's lips. "I thought I told you to tell me the truth."

"But that is the truth. As I was saying, my mom's sick and she needs to get to the doctor, and we don't got no money, so—"

Michael looked like he was about to bust a blood vessel. "Shut the fuck up before I shut you up permanently," he growled.

The boy's mouth snapped shut.

"I don't have time for this shit." Michael's gaze swept the storage room, landing on some sort of meat mallet. "Hand me that, Dom," he said, pointing at the object before folding up his switchblade and putting it away.

I picked up the tool and passed it to Michael.

"I need something to put his hand on." Michael pointed to a step ladder in the corner. "There. Get me that."

Mario retrieved the ladder, opening it beside the chair.

"Put your hand on it," Michael ordered.

Face twisted, the boy looked up at me like I would help him.

"If you spread out your fingers wide, he might just crush one or two," I said helpfully.

"You can't... I don't..." the kid stammered, looking from me to Michael.

"Oh, he can," Mario replied. "And he will. I've seen him do it more times than I can count. If smashing bones was an Olympic sport, he'd have the gold."

I moved forward and grabbed the kid's hand, tugging it away from his body. He resisted, but it only took me seconds to get his hand splayed out on the step ladder. "Here?" I asked.

My brother nodded and raised the mallet. "On the count of three. One. Two."

"Wait," the kid said, his voice cracking.

Mallet still prepared to strike, Michael eyed the kid. "Wait for what?"

"Can I talk now?" he asked.

Michael eyed him. "Depends on what you have to say. Better not waste my time."

"I… I don't know his name, but I can tell you what he looks like."

"Who?" I asked.

"The dude who hired me." The kid tried to pull his hand back, but I held it firm.

"Start talkin'," Michael growled.

"D-d-dark hair. Not much taller than me. Maybe five foot five. Big guy."

"That's all you got?" Michael took a couple practice swings before lining up again. "You just described half the men in Vegas. Better give me more than that."

The kid started trembling. "Guy who sells me blow told me about the gig. Said I'd score a free bag if I messed with a couple of cars in the lot."

"Messed with how?" I asked.

"Slash a few tires, bust a couple windows, nuthin' serious. It was all for fun. He said nobody would get hurt, and I needed a fix."

His employer wanted to send us a message *and* make us look bad in front of our guests. We needed to find out who it was.

"Y-y-you see? Whatever you think it is, it's not. I was just tryin' to score a gram."

Michael was still poised to strike. "Who's your dealer?" he asked.

"I don't know his name," the kid said.

Michael made eye contact with me and I saw what he was about to do. He swung as I released my hold on the kid's hand. The mallet slammed down with a bone-breaking crunch.

"What the fuck?!" the kid shouted, cradling his injured hand. His pinky was noticeably flatter than the rest of his fingers. "Goddamn, you didn't have to—"

"Who's your dealer?" Michael asked.

"I told you I don't know his name."

"Dom," Michael said, nodding to the kid. My brother could be a scary motherfucker when he needed to be.

When I reached for his hand, he shook it away from me. "I'm tellin' you the truth, dude. I don't know his name. Nobody does. He just goes by Lucky."

I only knew of one Lucky in Vegas. Giacomo "Lucky" Borghi was *the* point man for the Durante's drug operation. Could it possibly be that easy to connect this kid with our enemies?

"Where's your drop point?" I asked.

"The Columbian. Lucky has a room there."

Yep. The Columbian was one of the two casinos owned and operated by Maurizio Durante himself. No doubt he'd ordered his drug man to find a junkie desperate and stupid enough to mess with us. If the kid got caught, he could finger Lucky, but that wouldn't hold water with the families. They'd need more than some junkie's confession. But something still didn't make sense.

"Why him?" I asked, gesturing at the kid. "If Maurizio wanted to make us look bad in front of the De Luccas, why not just send soldiers and shoot the place up?"

"Maurizio's crazy, not stupid. He's not gonna start a war with the De Lucca's. Just wants us to look incompetent."

Since we hadn't been able to sniff out Chains and his crew, our family's competency and power were already under question. We couldn't afford for anything else to go wrong.

"Did he do any damage before the men nabbed him?" I asked.

Mario nodded. "Sliced two of the tires of De Lucca's Lamborghini. I already called for replacements. If Triple A isn't out there now, they will be soon. We'll have the whole thing handled before dinner lets out."

"Good." Michael handed me the mallet. "I better get back to the party. Dom, show our uninvited guest out and make sure he's dissuaded from making another appearance."

"Oh no, I wouldn't do that," the kid insisted. "If you let me go I swear you'll never see me near this restaurant again."

Michael shook his head and walked out the door.

"Just shut up," I said, untying the rope to free him.

"You're not gonna kill me, are you?" he asked. "I mean I don't know anything and even if I did, I wouldn't tell anybody and—"

I jerked the kid to his feet. "I said shut up."

Mario and I took the kid out the back and released him.

"You're really not gonna kill me?" he asked. "When I turn around, you won't shoot me in the back, will ya?"

I chuckled. No point in killing him since he already had one foot in the grave. He just didn't know it yet. "Look kid, I'm the least of your worries. You just rolled over on the craziest son-of-a-bitch in this city. If you don't leave town, you'll be dead by morning."

He looked like he was gonna say more, so I pulled my sig out of my pocket and turned off the safety. "Now, get out of here before I change my mind."

The kid took off.

"Think he's smart enough to take your advice?" Mario asked as he lit up a cigarette.

I watched the kid disappear around a corner as I slid a smoke out of the pack and joined him. "Not a chance. But if I know my brother, he slipped out to put a man on the kid. Hopefully when the Durantes pop him, they'll lead us back to whoever issued the order."

A Triple A truck drove into the parking lot. Mario flagged them down and we led them to the Lamborghini with the slashed tires. They got to work as we leaned against the building and watched. Grateful for the reprieve from Valentina, I let my mind wander to Annetta. Thinking about her plump lips and her round ass served as a nice escape from the evening. I wondered how she'd held up tonight and what she was doing after work. Glancing at my watch, I realized she was probably already gone for the night.

"Damn," I said, snuffing out my smoke.

"What?" Mario asked, glancing around.

"Annetta. I forgot about getting her home."

He chuckled and shook his head. "The engagement dinner's over, Dom. You don't have to look out for her anymore."

Right. My babysitting duties were over. I should feel relieved, but instead I felt… disappointed. Didn't matter, though. Father had already set his sights on hitching me to Valentina, and Annetta didn't seem like the kind of girl who'd be a side piece. Whatever had been developing between us needed to end. Reluctantly resigned to walk away from her, I lit up another cigarette and watched the crew finish up with Don De Lucca's Lamborghini.

CHAPTER TEN
Dominico

WITH THE ENGAGEMENT party out of the way, the family went back to business as usual. Since no one had unearthed Chains and his crew, Father was still on the warpath, making it clear our heads were going to roll if we didn't bring him theirs. Michael and I split up to increase our chances, me riding with Mario while my brother teamed up with one of Carlo's soldiers. Regardless, it took five more days before we found Chains.

I knew Chains was dead before we got the call. I knew it because we'd been watching his usual haunts, including his mom's house and his girlfriend's apartment, and hadn't caught so much as a whiff of him. We had, however, tapped into her phone and listened as his mom called the cops, the news, local politicians, and anyone else who might be able to help her find her missing son.

See, Chains was Italian. And any respectable Italian man would tell you that if his life was in danger he might go a couple of weeks without getting laid, but there's no way he'd make his mom worry like that. He would find a way to let her know he was okay. To do otherwise would be downright disrespectful, and she'd never let him hear the end of it.

Chains's body showed up in a landfill northeast of Vegas. Carlo called me and Michael in and sent us up to look it over and see if anything on him would point back to the Durante's. Chains's killer had dumped his body naked, though, and judging by his ripe condition, more than a week ago.

Michael kicked the body over, and we both almost lost our lunch. I covered my nose with my jacket and got a brief look at the corpse before nausea forced me to turn away. The gunshot wound on the side of his head looked like it could have been self-inflicted. Of course, Chains would have had to drive his own bare ass to the dump before his brains leaked out of the hole, so Michael and I ruled out suicide.

We searched the area for clues, finding the body of the tire-slashing kid Mario had found outside of the engagement dinner. Michael had put a tail on the kid, but we'd found the soldier dead in his car a few days ago. They must have made him when they popped the kid.

"Come on," Michael said, sounding defeated.

We climbed back in his car and both lit up. Since Chains was the only participant in the hit we'd been able to identify, we were screwed. Knowing our old man would freak the hell out about the literal dead end, we headed for Carlo's house. He listened to our story, poured himself two fingers of cognac, and chain-smoked Cubans for five minutes before calling Father. Our old man screamed so loudly Carlo had to hold the phone away from his ear.

When Father's rant finally ended, Carlo put the receiver back to his cheek and said, "Yes, Boss," before hanging up. Then he turned toward us. "Whoever did this is covering their tracks. Chains blabbed, so they took him out. Just like the kid you found. This situation is making us look like goddamn amateurs, and we need to get it straightened out."

Yeah, we did, but Michael and I were fresh out of leads. We left Carlo's office feeling frustrated and hopeless.

"I'm spent," Michael said, rubbing a hand down his face. "I can't wait till we find the bastards who did this, but I need a minute. There's a couple soldiers working on a job I want in on. I'm gonna peel off and join them for it. I gotta do something that gets results before I blow my own goddamn brains out."

Father wanted us back out there pounding the pavement, but I needed a break too. "Yeah, I got a couple of things to take care of as well," I said. I had nothing to do, but needed to be away from him and the family for a while.

Michael dropped me off at the casino, where I climbed into my Porsche and took off. I had no destination in mind, but put myself on autopilot and drove. I didn't even realize where was going until I turned down Annetta's street. It had been days since I'd last seen her, and although I knew I needed to stay away, I couldn't stop thinking about her. Even as I parked in front of her house, I told myself I shouldn't be there. A better man would have driven away, but I've never claimed to be a good guy.

Her father's beat-up Chevy truck wasn't in the driveway. Knowing he was probably working, I sat in the car and fiddled with my radio. I'd made the oldies station one of my presets after that first drive with Annetta, so I turned it on. The DJ was taking requests, and someone called in the song "Could It Be I'm Falling in Love" by the Spinners. Nice beat, dumb ass mushy song full of all sorts of romantic bullshit.

Love was a fantasy no mobster could afford, but I'd settle for getting laid. I killed the engine and got out, still unsure of what I planned to do. Ready to wing it if she answered, I knocked and waited.

Annetta opened the door wearing a pair of tight blue jeans with rips down the legs and a white sweater hanging off one shoulder. It showed about an inch of her flat stomach and made it practically impossible to focus on her eyes and not gawk at her body. I'd always suspected she was perfect under her baggy chef uniform, but damn, the girl was hot. I wanted to see the rest of her.

"Hey, Dom." Her tone was cold, standoffish. "What are you doing here?"

Not the reception I'd been hoping for, but her question was valid since I still had no idea. "I stopped by to see how you're doing."

She crossed her arms. "Uh... fine, thanks."

Realizing I needed a better reason than the one I'd given her, I added, "How's work? How are you liking the restaurant?"

"Oh, that." Her shoulders relaxed, and she let out a breath. "It's going well. Everyone's been great and helpful, and now that the dinner's over, the environment is way more relaxed."

"Good to hear. Are you still getting enough hours?"

She arched an eyebrow at me. "Why do you ask?"

I shrugged.

"You know I'm not really good at small talk, Dom." She leaned against the door frame. "So why don't you just tell me why you're really here."

She wanted to know? All right, I'd tell her. I wasn't some goddamn chicken who'd back down. Besides, I still wanted to see the rest of her smokin' body. "I missed you."

Her eyes widened for a second, and then her brow furrowed. She looked down at my feet and asked, "Why would you miss me?"

Why'd she have to make this so damn complicated? "I don't know. I just... enjoy being around you, okay? I miss our drives."

"Then tell me the truth. If you work security, why don't I ever see you at the restaurant."

I scratched at the two-day scruff on my chin and admitted, "I'm not employed at the restaurant. I do some security work, but only for my family."

"And your family is the one who rented out the restaurant?" she asked.

I nodded.

"For your engagement party?" she asked.

I choked. "What? No. Definitely not."

"But what about the girl in the pink dress?" she asked. "She's not your fiancée?"

Wondering who the hell told Annetta about Valentina, I said, "Nope. Just a family friend."

"Really? Because she's already picking out wedding colors."

I didn't want to lie to Annetta, but I didn't want to push her away with the truth, either. How could I make her understand without telling her about my fucked-up family? I sighed, hoping she'd be able to hear and see my honesty. "Not if I have anything to say about it."

Annetta studied me, keeping her arms crossed in front of her. I halfway expected her to slam the door in my face, but she didn't. "I missed you too," she finally whispered.

She did? And she wasn't gonna be all bitchy about Valentina? Thinking I'd hit the lottery, I decided to push my luck. "Been a rough couple of days and I just wanted to... to hang out. You feel like goin' somewhere? Maybe grab a bite to eat?"

She chewed on her lip and looked over her shoulder back in the house.

"If you're busy, we can do it another time." I wanted to be with her right then, but would settle for a rain check over an outright rejection.

"I was supposed to go out with a friend, but she ditched me for a date with your friend."

"Huh?"

"Mario. He stole my friend Adona today."

Surprised because Mario tended to be a bit shy around the ladies, I grinned. "She must have asked him."

"Knowing her, it was more like a clobbering over the head. I don't know if he's ready for a girl like Adona. Poor guy. I tried to warn him."

The idea of Mario being accosted by some overly-zealous girl only widened my grin. "It'll be good for him. And funny. I wish I could be a fly on the wall for that date."

The sound of Annetta's laughter made me feel better than I had in days. "Yeah, not me. She'll tell me all about it later. Unfortunately."

"So, what do you say? Let's get out of here and go do something."

"I just... let me turn off the television and leave Papa a note." She headed into the house, and then paused. "You wanna come in?"

"Sure."

I followed Annetta into the small, single-level house. A brown recliner sat beside a blue floral sofa in the modest living room. Everything looked clean, but worn. Residual food smells lingered, and books and magazines were stacked on the coffee table, giving a comfortable feel to the place. I tried to imagine what it would be like to grow up here, but couldn't. It was way too different from my parents' house.

Annetta turned off the small television and invited me to have a seat. "Is what I'm wearing okay?" she asked, eyeing my suit.

I definitely didn't want her to change. "Perfect. You look great."

"Thanks." The slightest hint of pink colored her cheeks as she headed for the adjoining dining room, returning with a pad of paper and a pen. "Can I get you anything to drink? Water? A coke?"

"No thanks. I'm good."

She sat beside me on the sofa and used the coffee table to scribble out a note. I don't know what kind of perfume she was wearing, but I wanted to roll around in it. To roll around in her. I leaned closer and breathed her in.

She turned and eyed me. "You said you're not engaged, but the girl in the pink dress... is she your girlfriend?"

"Nope." And it was encouraging that Annetta cared. Maybe I'd be getting lucky tonight after all. I held up my right hand. "I, Dominico, do solemnly swear I am unattached." And I silently vowed to stay that way for as long as possible.

She giggled. "Good to know. It's not like I'm assuming this is a date or anything, but I'm not that girl... the one who dates guys with girlfriends." Her cheeks turned bright red. "Again, not dating, but I mean... never mind."

You bet your sweet ass it's a date.

I rubbed her back. "Annetta, you wanna go out on a date with me?"

Instead of replying, she signed her name to the note and set it on the coffee table. Her cheeks were still red, and I got the feeling she was trying to figure out how to respond. I didn't want to give her a chance to reject the idea, so I leaned against her and gently took her chin in my hand. Her skin felt smooth and soft as I turned her face to look at me. Eyes wide and breath quickened, she watched me. I pressed my lips to hers. Soft, plump, inviting, they swept me into her. Deepening the kiss, before I knew it, my arms were around her. She sighed, and I almost lost my shit and attacked her. My hands drifted up her sweater, but she stopped me. I pulled back and watched her, hoping I hadn't completely blown it by trying to feel her up.

"You taking me out on a date or what?" she asked, bolting to her feet and grabbing a jacket from the coat tree by the front door. Her lips were even plumper and her eyes looked wild. I wanted to scoop her up and go find her bedroom, but knew she wouldn't appreciate that. Not yet at least.

Thankful for the suit jacket that would hide my erection, I adjusted myself as I stood and followed her out the door.

CHAPTER ELEVEN
Annetta

I HAD TO be losing my mind. That's the only explanation I could come up with for agreeing to go on a date with Dominico. I'd seen the girl in the pink dress, heard her plans for a future with him, and could tell he was hiding something from me. Maybe lots of somethings. The guy had to be loaded. Each suit he wore probably cost more than my entire wardrobe, and he seemed to wear a new one every day. And he was dangerous. When we were making out on my sofa, I felt something hard on his left hip. A gun? It sure felt like it. Rich, deadly, and possibly taken, yet his kiss had practically melted my panties right off. I had no idea that was actually a thing until Dominico came into my life, but my panties... I needed to hit the restroom and see if they'd combusted.

Get it together, Annetta!

What was wrong with me? I was not the stupid girl who fell for the hot bad boy. That would be my friend Adona for you. I, on the other hand, was the smart, sensible one with a plan for the future that I intended to follow. But one look at

Dominico, and all sensible thoughts flew straight out the window. Which explained why I'd agreed to go on a date to an undisclosed location with a guy who was the very definition of armed and dangerous.

"Where are we going again?" I asked.

Dominico chuckled. "Nice try, but it's still a surprise."

"What if I don't like surprises?"

He parked and gave me a cocky smile before his fiery gaze took over, drifting south to scorch my legs and then headed north to consume my breasts. With one look, he had ignited my entire body, and I didn't know whether to slap him or stop, drop, and roll.

"You scared?" he asked.

Terrified, but there was no way I was going to admit to that. While I tried to come up with a response, Dominico circled the car, opened my door, and hefted me toward him. Our bodies collided and he wrapped his arms around me, drawing in for another deep kiss before releasing me.

I was still struggling to calm down my breathing as he spun me around, covering my eyes with his hands as his hard chest pressed against my back.

"Don't worry, I got you," he whispered against my cheek.

Strangely enough, I trusted him. He ushered me out of the sun and traffic noise, into air conditioning and quiet classical music. We took several more steps before he helped me slide into a booth and uncovered my eyes.

Dominico's smiling face was the first thing I saw. "You good?" he asked.

Better than good. Everything about the man was thrilling and mysterious, bringing all my senses to life. I nodded. "Where are we?"

"Not yet. Give me two more minutes. Wait here."

He left me at the booth and headed straight for a man in a suit. The two bent their heads together and I checked out my surroundings. Stylish aluminum ceiling, hunter-green walls, numerous gilded mirrors, crystal chandeliers, and a gorgeous oak bar gave the place an old-fashioned feel. The restaurant was small, and the menus were black with no logo. They probably had a sign out front, but we'd parked in the back.

"Can I get you something to drink, ma'am?" a man behind me asked.

I swiveled my head to find the waiter watching me. Yes, a drink would help my nerves. I ordered a Mai Tai and then realized I had no idea what Dominico would want. Thankfully he appeared and ordered a beer before taking his place across from me.

"What is this place?" I asked.

He grinned, clearly having way too much fun with my ignorance. "Don't you like surprises?" he asked.

"But we're here. It's time for the big reveal."

He shook his head. "Hey, when I do something, I do it right."

Before I could figure out how to respond to that statement, a loud alarm sounded.

"What's that?" I asked, covering my ears.

Dominico smiled. "You'll see. Or hopefully, you won't."

The alarm ended, and moments later, a family hurried past the bar entrance. "I told you it wasn't in there," the forty-something mom said. "If you guys would listen to me every once in a while, we would've won."

Neither the dad nor the two teenage boys replied. Instead, they kept their heads down and sped up their pace, looking embarrassed as they passed.

"It's a win or lose thing?" I asked.

Dominico nodded and looked away, but not before I caught his smile.

Fine. If he didn't want to give up any clues about what we were doing, I would pump him for other information. "You never got the chance to tell me about your family," I said, drawing his attention back to me.

The server brought our drinks. Dominico held up a finger and took a sip. "That was intentional," he admitted. "You don't really want to hear about them."

"Yes, I do. Do you have any siblings besides Michael and your sister who's about to get married?"

"Nope. Just the three of us."

I could tell by the way his smile disappeared that he didn't want to talk about them, but I wasn't willing to let it go. I needed to know something about him. "Your parents still married?"

"Yep." He looked at me like I was crazy, which told me divorce wasn't an issue in his world.

"Nice. What are they like?"

"You're like a dog with a bone," he said.

"Is getting to know you really that bad?"

He chuckled and played with his glass. "Well played. Mamma is nice. Smart. Forever trying to shove food down our throats. It's a miracle we're all not three hundred pounds. You'd like her."

I giggled. "Is she a good cook?"

"Oh, the best."

I arched an eyebrow.

"Present company excluded," he amended. "But if you ever tell her I said that, I will deny it."

Mimicking the gesture he'd shown me the first night he took me home, I held up my right hand and said, "Scouts honor."

"You're tellin' me *you* were a Boy Scout?" he asked.

I leaned back in my chair and threw up my hands. "No more than you were."

He held my gaze for a moment before breaking into a smirk. "Touché."

Dominico's mother was a housewife and his father was some sort of businessman. I made a mental note to ask Papa if he knew anyone in the Mariani family so I could find out more, but was unable to squeeze anything else out of Dominico before a man approached and introduced himself.

"My name is John and I'll be your guide for this evening. Are you ready to begin the challenge?"

A challenge? I raised my eyebrows at Dominico and he nodded. We grabbed our drinks and followed John out of the restaurant and down the hall. He opened a door and waved for us to precede him into a large room decorated and furnished in an early 1900s motif, before handing us each a spy glass and a Sherlock Holmes style hat. Then he started in on the spiel.

"This is the escape room, which means your goal will be to escape it. To do this, you'll need to solve five riddles that will each give you one of the numbers on this lock." He pointed at the keypad on the wall. "Enter all five numbers and the door will unlock and you will win."

A little thrill ran up my spine. I'd heard of places like this before, but had never been in one. I scanned the room as he continued speaking, wondering where all the clues were hiding.

"In a moment, I'll hand you your first clue," John continued. "It will lead you to the first number and your clue to the next. You will have sixty minutes to solve the lock and escape the room before an alarm sounds, letting the entire establishment know you failed."

Well that explained a lot. "You shame the losers?" I asked.

Dominico grinned. "Amateurs. Don't worry, we've got this."

John didn't look nearly as certain about our sleuthing abilities as he handed over our first clue, wished us luck, and then let himself out. The door clicked locked behind him, and the second hand on the giant wall clock started ticking.

"Have you done this before?" I asked.

"No, but how hard can it be?" Dominico read the first clue aloud—a riddle blatantly pointing us to the fireplace. We searched the hearth until we found a loose stone, which pulled away to reveal another piece of paper. This one had the number six and a clue on it.

"See? Piece of cake," Dominico said, suddenly in my space. "Nothing to worry about. In fact, I think we should talk about a reward." His gaze was intense as he draped an arm around my waist and pulled me closer.

I swallowed past the lump in my throat, both afraid and excited. "Reward?"

"Yeah. If we win—when we win—you owe me a second date."

And what if I was the one who figured out all the clues? But since I wanted a second date with him, I didn't question his methods, instead nodding in acceptance. "Deal."

He smirked and gave me a quick peck on the cheek before reading the clue aloud.

Each clue grew increasingly difficult to decipher. Not only that, some of them purposely misled us. I would have sworn the third clue pointed to the window, but when I pulled back the heavy drape, a giant fake spider jumped out at me. I screamed so loud I'm sure the entire building heard. Dominico rushed to help me, but when he saw what had happened, he laughed until I thought he was going to pee his pants. Once my heart stopped racing, I laughed as well. We worked together and eventually figured out the riddle, but I was much more cautious searching for the fourth clue.

By the time we had the fifth riddle in hand, we only had six minutes left. We read it over and over, looking for patterns and searching for deeper meaning, but it didn't make sense. I was scanning the paper, hoping to shed some light on the problem, when I realized the first letter of each word spelled out "red lamp."

"Red lamp! Red lamp!" I shouted. We had barely over a minute and still had to punch in the code.

Dominico rushed for the end table with the red lamp and searched for the clue. When he couldn't find it, he ripped off the shade and tossed the lamp on the floor. Surprisingly, it didn't break.

"What are you—you can't—"

Before I could even form a coherent sentence, he jumped on the lamp, smashing it to pieces. I watched, too shocked to speak, as he bent and removed the final piece of paper from the debris and laid it on the coffee table.

"Read me the numbers," he said, running toward the keypad.

That snapped me out of my stupor. I leaned over the table and recited the digits as he punched them in. The door clicked open only seconds before the clock ran out.

"Ohmigod, we did it!" I said, looking from Dominico to the smashed lamp. I still couldn't believe he'd broken it, but the adrenaline had me all amped up.

"Let's go get our prizes," he said, draping an arm over my shoulders.

"We get prizes?" I asked.

"Of course we do. But my real reward is coming later. Thank you, Annetta."

His tone was somber. Confused as to why he'd be thanking me, I stared up at him. "For what?" I asked.

He played with one of my curls. "For coming with me. For this. I needed it."

His eyes were almost black. Mysterious and a little frightening, they made me feel like Alice, straddling a bottomless pit full of magical potential. This Wonderland might kill me, but it would be one hell of a fun ride.

"I did too," I admitted.

Someone cleared their throat by the door. "I apologize for interrupting," John said, opening the door the rest of the way. "But they are ready for you."

"Who?" I asked.

"The photographer. We need pictures—lots of pictures— to immortalize the night we kicked Escape Room C's ass!" Dominico said as he slid away from me, grabbing my hand.

We followed John down another hall, where we were shown into a small room with an early 1900s backdrop. Props were everywhere. We dressed in overcoats with attached capes and the silly little hats Sherlock Holmes wore, which the photographer informed us were called deerstalkers. We were each awarded a magnifying glass and a pipe for our win, and we spent the next ten minutes egged on by an overzealous cameraman to explore every ridiculous pose we could.

"Come on, give her a kiss," he heckled.

Dominico pecked my cheek.

"You call that a kiss?" the cameraman hooted. "Who is she? Your sister?"

Dominico didn't seem like the type to turn down a challenge, and he certainly rose to this one. Slipping his arm behind my back, he pulled me closer and set my world on fire again with his own unique blend of passion and power that made my knees buckle. I leaned into him and the contact threatened to burn up my entire body. The camera flash brought us both back to reality. We pulled apart and breathlessly stared at one another. He looked as affected as I felt.

Dominico pulled himself together first. "Excuse me for a moment," he said, heading for the cameraman.

The two of them looked over the pictures while I removed my costume and tried to get my emotions under control. Dominico returned, minus his costume and with a fistful of pictures, and led me out of the room back to the bar where we were cheered, given gifts, and bought drinks.

"Turns out winning is pretty rare," he explained. "We're kinda a big deal right now."

"There was no hidden compartment in the lamp, was there?"

"Nope. If I hadn't broken it, we would have failed."

"That's pretty sneaky of them," I said.

He shrugged. "This is Vegas. Everything's fixed, and nothing's ever what it seems."

Which was exactly what I was afraid of.

CHAPTER TWELVE
Dominico

I DIDN'T EVEN get to finish my first victory drink with Annetta before my pager interrupted our date. In hindsight, I was lucky it didn't go off while we were trapped in the escape room since both Carlo and my father expected their pages to be returned immediately. Still, the damn thing's intrusive beeping made me want to smash it against the wall. Who knew, maybe there'd be a clue inside it as to how to get my life back.

I excused myself from the table and called Carlo to see what he wanted. Carlo never gave away too much over the phone, but after years of working with him, his code was easier to crack than the Escape Room's had been. A couple of his soldiers had gotten a bead on possible accomplices of Chains's, and Carlo wanted me to come in so he could give me the details. I promised to meet him at his home office as soon as possible and hung up.

"Is everything okay?" Annetta asked when I returned to the table.

No, everything wasn't okay. I'd been enjoying my time with her, and had been hoping her old man would still be gone when I dropped her off. Maybe she'd invite me in and I'd get to see what was under that sweater. But now I needed to pump the brakes on all that to hunt down the guys who'd killed my family's soldiers.

"I got called into work, so I'm gonna have to take you home."

"Okay," she said before sucking down her drink.

Hollywood always made mobsters look like players who spent every night in the bed of a different broad. I don't know which family they got their information from, but Marianis... we worked our asses off. Most nights, I'd settle for sleeping in any bed. Hell, even a sofa would do. But if you didn't hustle, you didn't eat. Not only that, your capo would see you as dead weight and eventually trim the fat.

Because of my erratic and heavy work schedule, I didn't go out much. When I did, most of my dates ended with my pager going off, which girls never seemed to take too well. Yeah, Annetta sounded disappointed, but at least she didn't whine or complain or accuse me of making shit up. She just grabbed her purse and stood, ready to go.

"I really do have to work," I said, wondering if she thought I was brushing her off.

She gave me an amused smile. "Do you expect me to beg you to blow off your job and stay?"

Yeah, I kinda had been. "I would if I could. I hope you know that. This has been nice."

"I know. I get it. No biggie. I had fun too, but it's time to get back to reality."

With that, she headed toward the exit. We laughed about our escape room adventure on the drive, and then I dropped her off at her front door. Her old man's truck was in the drive, so I wouldn't have gotten lucky even if Carlo hadn't called me in. Resigned to the shittiness of it all, I pulled Annetta in for one last kiss, beyond caring if her old man caught us. She tasted of the fruity drink she'd just downed, and I wanted nothing more than to find out what the rest of her tasted like. No time, and I didn't know when I'd have another free afternoon.

"My work schedule is nuts, so I'm not sure when I'll be able to do this again," I said.

Hurt flashed in her eyes, but she nodded and gave me a smile. "Thank you."

Maybe she did think I was ditching her after all. I tugged on her hand, drawing her attention back to me. "Don't forget that you owe me another date. I do plan on cashing that in. I'll call you to set it up."

A smile tugged at her lips. "You don't even have my number."

I rattled off the digits I'd memorized from her résumé.

"Wow, that's kinda stalkerish," she said, but her smile only widened. "Do you have a number?"

"Yeah, but I'm never home." I could give her my pager number, but Carlo monitored my pager log and I didn't want him to know about Annetta. At least not yet. Probably not ever.

*   *   *

Carlo lived in a modest, Southwestern stucco split-level house in a gated community. He could afford better, and my father had asked him to build closer to our home, but Carlo made it clear he preferred the humble home. As a Mustache Pete—an old school wiseguy—my uncle played his role like he played poker, cards close to his chest. Nothing about his home or his car even hinted at the kind of money he had to be worth. In fact, his home blended in with the upper middle-class community so well no outsider would believe the Mariani family underboss resided within.

I got out of my car and the smell of cigarette smoke drew my attention to the garage where Michael and a few guys from Carlo's crew were hidden from the view of the street. They greeted me, snuffed out their cigarettes, and we all headed in together. Carlo had a new live-in housekeeper, Constanza, who Michael knew from high school. She'd been a year ahead of him, but her small frame and sweet face made her look like she should be studying for a final rather than taking care of a capo.

"Hello Michael. Dominico. Gentlemen," she said, welcoming us in. Since Michael and I were family, she always made sure to address us individually as a show of respect.

"Hello, Constanza. Is he ready for us?" Michael replied.

"Yes. Right this way, please."

She led us to Carlo's office as if we hadn't been there a million times before. It wasn't as big as his office at the casino, but the eight of us fit comfortably. He waited until everyone sat before starting in on business.

"Earlier today I got a call about three possible associates of Chains." Carlo gestured at two of his men. "David and Gian here tracked the men down, only to find their bodies stinking up the Dumpster behind an apartment building. Like Chains, they'd been stripped down and left with the garbage."

"Do they have any Durante ties?" Michael asked.

"That's where you guys come in. We have addresses and names now, so I need to see what you can find out about them. I want family, friends, work, everything. We need evidence that these assholes are connected to the Durantes before the Commission sends a *messaggero* in to make us keep the peace."

"A messaggero?" David asked.

David had blond hair and blue eyes. I'd met him in passing, but didn't care enough about him to learn his story: whether he'd married into the family or had been recruited. He clearly hadn't learned the language yet.

"A liaison who goes between the families to prevent war," Carlo replied. "A peacekeeper of sorts. They're supposed to open communication to help prevent… misunderstandings. Too many scrapes with the Durantes has gotten national attention, so the Commission recommended a messaggero to help us get it under control."

Recommended. Yeah, right. The Commission was like the national association of wiseguys, made up of the country's most powerful mobsters. They didn't make recommendations, they told us all what to do. Their number one goal was to protect their bottom lines, which meant there must have been enough media coverage about the Vegas happenings to make the meat eaters (corrupt cops) nervous about getting greased.

"We need to solve this problem and convince the Commission we don't need a messaggero," Carlo said. "We need to take out the Durantes."

"'Bout time," Gian replied, sounding way too enthusiastic. "The crew's been itchin' for some action."

"Those dumbasses are what's gotten us into this mess. No one touches the Durantes," Carlo growled. "At least not in a way that draws attention. Best relay that to the crew, because the next person who lands us on the news is gonna answer to me. We need to be more calculated about our attacks, so we're going to shift our focus to gathering information and funds. Keep hustling like you've been, but in addition to collecting information on Chains's crew, I want your ears to the ground about anything the Durantes are scheming. Any hits they're planning, any jobs they're working... Hell, if they start selling peanuts on the side of the road I want to hear about it before it happens. *Capisce?*"

"Yessir," we all replied.

"Good. We cripple them financially while this whole messaggero threat cools, then we strike. Now go get to work."

Carlo dismissed the others, directing me and Michael to stay. He splashed Cognac into three glasses, handing me and Michael each one before sitting behind his desk.

"Last thing we need right now is for this Commission rat to come 'round pokin' his nose in our business," he said. "We need to have this thing with the Durantes tied up with a mother-fuckin' bow before they come a snoopin'."

Problem was, we didn't have a damn thing under control. In addition to the recent hit, six of our warehouses and drop points had been attacked over the past four months. We'd also had soldiers jumped in broad daylight and one delivery interrupted midroute. Sure, we'd retaliated and gotten in a few of our own punches, but the odds were stacked against us. Still, this was Vegas, where anything could happen. Especially if you knew how to manipulate the odds.

"Which is why Father is recruiting help from California," I said.

"From anywhere he can get it," Carlo amended.

My old man was kind of an asshole, and not exactly known for his ability to make friends. He didn't play well with others, especially not other family bosses. "Do you think he'll be able to get what we need in time?"

"I learned long ago not to underestimate my brother," Carlo replied. "He always manages to surprise me. Sometimes that's even good."

Michael and I both nodded. The old man could be one volatile son-of-a-bitch, and the more power he gained the crazier and more violent it made him. Since he was unafraid to step on anyone to get to the top, weaker families aligned themselves with us so they wouldn't get trampled. Despite all his faults, Father was better than the alternative, though. Carlo said Maurizio had a screw loose, but everyone else referred to the Durante don as batshit crazy. Never to his face, though. Father was the first with the balls to go after Maurizio. Now he just needed the support to make it happen.

Someone knocked on Carlo's door.

Everyone in the room shifted, hands going to their pockets. We weren't exactly the most trusting lot.

"You expectin' someone?" Michael asked.

Constanza should have announced the visitor, and her absence put us all on alert.

"That's our secret weapon," Carlo replied, hurrying to open the door.

In walked a man I recognized, but couldn't place. My age, with dark hair and built like a professional lineman, his face split into a grin when his gaze met mine. "Dom. Good to see you again."

Then he wrapped me a crushing hug, one I remembered instantly. "Gino?"

He laughed. "In the flesh." He pulled away from me long enough to hug Michael. "Mike, how you two been?"

Gino Leone wasn't technically family, but his father had married my mom's cousin, so in a way, he sort of was. We used to be close, but I hadn't seen him since I was a kid when Mamma had taken me, Michael, and Abriana to spend the summer with Gino's family while Father broke ground in Vegas. Gino's parents had never been involved in the family business. His father worked at the Ford assembly plant, and his mom was a housewife. They lived in the small town of Claycomo, Missouri, and it had been the biggest shock of my life to spend a summer with them.

A year older than me, Gino had an older brother and two younger sisters. His brother had hung out with Michael all summer while Gino and I split our time between torturing and hiding from his little sisters. Father straightened out his business, and before school restarted, he sent for us. Gino and I had tried to keep in touch, but neither us of were big on writing letters, and long-distance phone calls were expensive. I never thought I'd see him again, especially not in Carlo's office.

"What are you doing here?" I asked.

His gaze slid to Carlo.

"He's working, Dom," Carlo replied. "Gino came to your old man for a job shortly after high school. He wanted to contact you, but I couldn't let him risk it."

"What?" Since high school? Four years, and nobody had told me. "Risk what?" I glanced at Michael, but he looked as surprised as I felt.

"Nobody but your father and I know who Gino is and why he's here." Carlo patted Gino on the back. "With no traceable family ties and coming from goddamn Missouri, he was perfect for the job we had for him."

Michael seemed to figure out what Carlo meant long before I did. He let out a breath and chuckled. "He's trying to get into the Durante family."

I looked from my brother to my uncle to my cousin, struggling to make sense of Michael's words.

"He *is* in," Carlo said, his voice heavy with pride. "Has been."

"Yep. I got made a few months ago."

"*You're* our guy inside the Durante family?" I asked, finally catching up to speed.

At his nod, my stomach felt ill. I liked Gino. If half the stuff we heard about Maurizio Durante was true, when they found out about him being a mole, Gino would be praying for death. And I'd never heard of a mole who didn't get caught eventually. Few survived the experience.

"Gino knows what he's doing," Carlo reassured me. "And he's gonna need to get out of here soon."

"Already?" I asked. Feeling like we had so much more to catch up on. I still couldn't believe he'd been in Vegas and I hadn't seen or run into him.

"Yeah, I asked Carlo if we could meet before shit got real crazy," Gino said. "I need a favor, Dom."

Sensing it would be a heavy one, I sat. "All right. What's up?"

CHAPTER THIRTEEN
Annetta

THE TELEVISION WAS blaring. I could hear it from the front porch before I even opened the door. Dominico kissed me good-bye and I let myself into the house, closing the door on my incredible dream date and running smack dab into reality. And reality smelled a lot like whiskey.

Papa was passed out in the recliner, work clothes and shoes still on, with an almost-empty fifth of bourbon on the coffee table beside him, an empty glass balanced on his thigh, and a framed photograph of my mother pressed against his chest. Papa liked his liquor, and during certain occasions he couldn't seem to find his way out of the bottle. Holidays were difficult, as was Mom's birthday, their wedding anniversary, and the date of her death.

I looked to my watch for the date. We were creeping up on the anniversary of Mom's death. I'd been so busy, I hadn't even realized it. Over the next several days, Papa would binge, and no amount of yelling or crying would keep him sober. Believe me, I've tried. I kept expecting Mom's passing to get easier on him, but each year seemed to be worse than the last.

After checking to make sure he was still breathing, I took the glass and the photo and set them both on the coffee table before trying to rouse him.

"Papa, come on, let's get you to bed," I said, swatting his thigh.

He didn't even stir, which told me how messed up he was. Even though I knew it wouldn't deter him, I put the lid on the last of the bourbon and hid it in the kitchen cabinet. At least he'd have to sober up enough to stumble in and find it if he wanted more.

Since I couldn't get him to bed, I grabbed one of his blankets and spread it over him, removing his glasses and kissing his forehead. These binges always made me feel more like the parent than the child. Still, there was something so beautifully heartbreaking about the way he still loved and missed my mom that I could never stay angry at him for too long. I wanted a love like that someday... hopefully without the tragedy, though.

With Papa taken care of, I locked up, grabbed the cordless phone, and headed to my bedroom. I'd just had the most incredible night of my life and knew Adona would want all the juicy details.

*   *   *

Dominico had set my world on fire, then left me to smolder and die out. Days passed without even a phone call from him. Hurt and angry about his abrupt absence from my life, I broke down and asked Papa what he knew about the Mariani family.

"Powerful family," Papa replied. "Why do you want to know?"

"Just curious," I lied.

Papa eyed me. It was only a few days past the anniversary of Mom's death, and he seemed mostly sober, but still had alcohol on his breath and seeping out his pores.

"This have anything to do with that boy who kept sniffin' around here and takin' you to work? The one with the expensive car and nice suits?"

I didn't want to lie, so I shrugged noncommittally.

"Haven't seen him around in a while," Papa noted.

"He was… helping out at the restaurant, but he's not at Antonio's anymore."

Papa scratched his chin. "That's too bad. A boy connected to the Mariani family could do a lot of good for you. You'd be well taken care of, luce dei miei occhi."

Papa had worked his entire life and still couldn't pay for the medical procedures that might have kept Mom alive, so I could understand why he wanted me to find a man who could take care of me. Blinded by all his own perceived shortcomings, he'd missed the most beautiful truth about himself. Mom made sure I knew how special he was, though. I was sixteen and kneeling beside her bed when she gripped my hand and referred to herself as lucky.

"Lucky? How can you say that?" I asked. She was in so much pain she could barely sit up, and the doctor said it wouldn't be long until she went to sleep and never woke again.

"Because we were happy."

We had been happy, but now we were struggling. We couldn't afford Mom's treatments and Papa had started drinking. The happiness from my childhood felt like it was unraveling.

"So many people go through life without feeling what your Papa and I feel for each other. I would trade a thousand years of not knowing him for the eighteen happy years we shared in a heartbeat. My hope is that someday you will know a love as strong as ours."

I frowned at the memory, knowing I wanted the same thing for myself. While we were in the Escape Room, I'd wondered if Dominico could be that guy for me… the one who made me so happy I felt lucky no matter what life threw at us. I didn't care about his family's money, I'd just liked being with him. But apparently, he didn't feel the same since the jerk couldn't even be bothered to call me back.

Resolved to put him out of my mind once and for all, I informed Papa, "I can take care of myself."

"Of course you can," he replied, without much confidence behind his words.

Frustrated, I let it drop, focusing instead on something Papa had said. He'd called the Marianis powerful. Why? "What do you mean by powerful family?" I asked, wondering if he'd validate my concerns. "Are they mafia?"

As an Italian, I'd been accused of being part of the mafia on more than one occasion. The stereotype angered me, but it was also somewhat true since my mom's side of the family had mob ties on the east coast. Truth be told, most Italians did have some sort of mob connection in their family.

Papa shrugged. "That's none of my business, so I wouldn't ask. As far as I know, they're successful businessmen who influence local politics."

Sounded like mobsters to me, and I didn't need that sort of complication in my life. I let the subject drop and headed to the kitchen where I could keep my hands busy and distract my mind from missing Dominico.

Over the next couple of weeks, I all but gave up on Dominico, pouring my time and energy into my job. With the dinner over, Collin had time to train me to do the position I'd been hired for. I cracked open my mom's old recipe binder and showed him what I could really do. I tweaked the restaurant's antipasto recipe, landed my roasted squash and beef carpaccio salad on the permanent menu, and added a few temporary dishes to the rotating daily specials. Positive feedback from customers earned me my first raise before my probation was even up.

Brandon and I worked a lot of the same shifts. His house was only a few blocks from mine, so, despite my insistence that the bus was a perfectly fine mode of transportation, he started giving me lifts to and from work. We went out for drinks twice, and the second time, he tried to snag a good-night kiss. I dodged, pretending not to know what he'd been about to do, and wrapped him in a quick hug before fleeing into the house. Brandon was great and all, but I felt nothing for him.

When he picked me up for work the next day, it was like the whole almost-kiss hadn't happened. Thankful things weren't awkward between us, I headed for his car.

"Why do you always do that?" Brandon asked, opening his door.

"Do what?" I climbed into the passenger's seat and buckled up.

"Look up and down the street like you're looking for someone," he replied. "You always do it before you get in."

It had been a little over three weeks since I'd seen or heard from Dominico. Most of me hoped I'd never see him again, but a tiny traitorous sliver of my heart still hoped he'd show up. I hadn't even realized I'd been watching for him. I shrugged. "Habit, I guess."

After work, Brandon asked me out again.

"I say we do something really crazy tomorrow since we're off," he said. "Let's go out to eat so someone else has to cook for us. Then we can see a movie... whichever one you want to catch."

Despite his easy smile, his eyes were hopeful. Adona was wrong, I wasn't oblivious to guys. Even if I was, a blind person could see that Brandon was into me, and regardless of his casual tone, dinner and a movie sounded like a date. It would be easy to like Brandon. He was cute and funny, and I enjoyed being around him, but he didn't set me on fire the way Dominico had. I didn't want to lead him on, but I didn't want to be alone for the rest of my life, either. Maybe some sort of spark could develop between us if we gave it enough time...

"I'm not sure," I replied.

His smile faltered.

My stomach twisted. I didn't want to hurt the guy, but I wasn't ready to say yes. "Can I call you later and let you know?" I asked.

"Of course," he said, parking in front of my house. "Take all the time you need, Annetta."

Confused and emotionally drained, I lumbered into the house and dropped my purse on the floor.

"Rough day?" Papa asked from his recliner.

Before I could answer, the phone rang.

He answered. "Hello. Yes. Who can I tell her is calling?" he asked. Then holding the phone toward me, he said, "It's for you. Says his name is Dom."

My heart did some stupid little flip in my chest and I all but growled at it. Three weeks. Three freaking weeks had passed and now he calls? Now that I had almost talked myself into moving on? No. Not happening, buddy. "Tell him I'm not here," I said.

"I'm sure he can hear you," Papa replied, looking point edly at the cordless phone dangling in the air between us. "Is he the one driving the Celica? Didn't he just drop you off?"

I about choked and reached for the phone. I didn't want to talk to Dominico, but I didn't want Papa telling him about Brandon, either. "Hello," I asked, heading for my room.

"Hey."

The sound made my knees wobbly. I closed my bedroom door and leaned against it, wondering what was up with my stupid body. Didn't it know what an inconsiderate asshole he was?

"Why are you calling?" I asked.

He let out a long, drawn-out sigh. "Because I'm a dumbass."

If he thought I was going to argue, he had another think coming. "Is that why you're calling now, or why you waited so long to call?" I asked.

"Hmm. The jury's still out on that one."

"Maybe you should call me when the jury makes up its mind. I'm guessing it'll take about three more weeks. Goodbye, Dom."

No matter what reactions my body had in response to hearing his voice, I refused to be led on by some player. I pulled the phone away and went to hit the end call button, but he yelled at me to wait.

I wanted to hang up and never think about him again. I also wanted him to have some legitimate excuse for not calling. How would I know if he did unless I heard him out?

"Annetta?" he asked.

Still undecided about whether or not to hang up on him, I put the phone back up to my ear and waited.

"I'm sorry I haven't called," he said with a deep sigh.

I didn't respond.

"I get that you're pissed. You should be. I just... I shouldn't be callin' at all." He sounded worn and frustrated.

I knew the feeling all too well. "Then why are you?" I asked.

"Because I'm weak and selfish, and even though I know I should, I can't seem to let you walk out of my life."

His honesty and the raw emotion in his voice rocked my resolve, making me admit to myself how much I'd missed him as well. Money didn't always mean an easy life, and Domincio sounded like he'd gone through the wringer. Still, I needed to protect my heart. He clearly wasn't the type of guy I could trust with it.

"Please talk to me," he pleaded, sounding more vulnerable than I would have thought possible. "It's been a rough past couple of weeks and... fuck it! I need to hear your voice."

That did me in. "What do you want me to say?" I relented.

"Anything. Just talk. How are you? How's work?"

I gave him a brief rundown on how well everything was going at Antonio's.

"Sounds like you're really enjoying it."

"I am, thanks."

"And how's your father?"

My gaze drifted to the door. We were on the other side of the anniversary of Mom's death and he seemed better—not necessarily sober, but coherent—today. "He's all right."

Awkward silence lingered between us, filling up with all the things I wish I could say. *Where were you? Why didn't you call? Are you okay?*

"What are you doing tonight?" he asked.

"Nothing. I just got home from work."

"Do you work tomorrow?"

Wondering where this line of questioning was going, I asked, "Why?"

"I know I fucked up by not calling you, Annetta, but I thought about you every single day."

Residual anger stirred within me. "Just not enough to call me."

"Too much to call you," he replied. "My life's complicated. I don't get the luxury of doing whatever the hell I want. But I missed you and... Damnit, I hate phones. Can I come pick you up?"

The question surprised me. "And take me where?" I asked.

"Anywhere you want to go."

Knowing I should decline the offer did not make me smart enough to do so. Especially when I had missed Dominco, too. "Will you talk to me? Tell me why you didn't call at least?"

"Annetta, I—"

The hesitancy in his voice told me all I needed to know. "Sounds like a no. Why don't you go ahead and give me a call if you change your mind?"

I tried to hang up for the second time.

"Wait! Annetta, listen. Okay, yes, I will tell you as much as I can."

Shocked that I was even considering it, I sniffed my hair, which still smelled like the restaurant. Before I could come to my senses, I said, "I can be ready in thirty minutes."

"Thank you. I'll be there." The relief in his voice chipped away the last of my resolve. Before I could say goodbye, he added, "Bring a swimsuit."

Wondering what the hell I'd signed up for, I clicked off the phone and headed for the shower.

CHAPTER FOURTEEN
Annetta

I WAS STILL drying my hair when Papa knocked on my bedroom door to let me know I had a guest. Butterflies danced in my stomach as I finished getting ready, stuffing my hot pink bikini in a bag. It was the most revealing piece of clothing I owned, and the idea of wearing it in front of Dominico did crazy things to my stupid stomach. Since I had no clue where we were going or what we were doing, I added a change of clothes and a brush to the bag.

Wearing a suit (as always), Dominico was seated on the sofa talking to Papa when I emerged from my room. He stood and looked me over, his eyes widening at the summer dress I wore.

"Is this okay?" I asked. I'd selected the dress because it made me feel sexy and I wanted to remind him I was still the girl he'd made out with in the escape room, but I felt suddenly self-conscious. What if he was taking me somewhere nice? "You didn't say where we were going."

"Perfect." He smiled. "You look great."

My cheeks heated as I thanked him.

He held up a bouquet of orange Gerber daisies. "I got these for you."

Unprepared for him to be sweet, my mind struggled to reconcile the jerk who hadn't called me for three weeks with the Dominico before me, the kind man I knew him to be. "Thanks, they're beautiful." I took the flowers into the kitchen to find a vase. Once they were arranged and set on the table, I followed him out the door.

"Have a good time," Papa called out from his chair.

"Your father is nice," Dominico said. "I think he likes me."

Since I didn't feel like letting him know that Papa only cared that he'd be able to support me, I nodded. "Yeah, he's great."

"You look incredible." Dominico watched me out of the corner of his eye as he revved the Porsche to life. "I mean it."

"Thank you." I'd never been good at taking compliments, so I hurried to change the subject. "Where are we going?"

"Another surprise." He stopped at the end of the block and turned to look at me. "Thanks again for coming with me. I know I don't deserve it, but I can't tell you how much it means."

He sounded vulnerable again. Something big must have happened in the three weeks we'd been apart for him to be so real with me. Making a mental note to pump him for information later, I nodded and answered truthfully. "I missed you too."

He shifted back into gear and took my hand, lifting it to kiss my knuckles. We drove for a while in comfortable silence before he parked in the driveway of a nice two-story house in Henderson. After opening my door, he popped the trunk and grabbed a duffle bag.

"You live here?" I asked, excited to finally be getting some information on him.

"No. Mario's family does. I'm keeping an eye on it for them while they're out of town." He unlocked the front door and let us in. The place was gorgeous. Marble entryway, high ceilings, hardwood floors. I followed Dominico into a living room that was about the size of my entire house. Stylish leather furniture was arranged around a beautiful contemporary rug, all angled toward a gorgeous stone fireplace.

"Nice pad," I said, spinning around to take it all in.

He nodded and carried the bags past the living room into the kitchen. "What do you like on your pizza? There's a great pizzeria not far from here. Thought I'd call us in an order."

I shrugged, buzzing with entirely too much energy to be hungry. "I like pretty much everything. Surprise me?"

"You got it," he said with a smile. "Can I get you a beer or a glass of wine?" He peeked into the refrigerator. "They have a decent Riesling. It's kinda like those fru-fru drinks you always get."

I giggled. "Fru-fru drinks, huh?"

He already had the corkscrew working. He splashed some into a glass and offered it to me. "Try it."

Fruity wine sounded fabulous. Especially since the way Dominico was looking at me had my stomach twisted in knots. I needed to relax. "Mario's family isn't gonna be upset about us drinking up their wine?" I asked, accepting the glass.

The look he gave me made me feel ridiculous for even asking such a thing. "No. They won't care what I touch. And when the maid comes in, she'll restock it."

"Well then." Feeling completely out of my element, I held the glass up in a mock toast, "Bottoms up."

I couldn't believe I'd said something so stupid. Why did my nerves always turn me into a dork? Desperate to settle myself down, I drained the glass and nodded for him to pour me more. He filled my glass and grabbed a beer for himself before leading me out to the patio, where he stripped off his jacket and tie, draping both over a chair. With his jacket off, my gaze was drawn to the gun holstered around his waist. Watching me, he removed it and set it on the table.

"I know you have questions," he said, sitting on the wicker couch and tugging me down beside him. "And I appreciate that you're not freaking out on me. I… there's a lot of shit I can't tell you. My job's pretty top secret and demanding, and sometimes I have to disappear for a while."

The mob. He worked for the mafia, and I suspected he was high up in his family. He didn't have to tell me, because I already knew. I did, however, need him to be honest with me.

"I know what you do, Dom," I said, still eyeing the weapon. "I'm not stupid."

He chuckled, relaxing his shoulders. "I know you're not, and I figured you knew, which is why I tried to stay away from you. I don't usually date. It's impossible to reach me and work often calls me away, as you've seen. I had a great time with you on our last date, but I don't want to hurt you. I don't want you to expect something I can't give you. You understand?"

Not really. It felt like he was breaking up with me, but we weren't even together. My chest constricted as I stared at his tortured expression, wishing I could do something to help him while simultaneously plotting his demise if he'd brought me here just to tell me goodbye. Needing to steady my nerves, I downed the rest of my wine.

"I really like you," he said, sounding amused and a little nervous as he watched me set the empty glass on the table beside his gun. "When I dropped you off that night after our date… everything went to shit on the job front. Made me realize I can't… I don't have the time to be in a relationship. And it's not fair to you. I tried to leave you alone, but I couldn't stay away. I can't stop thinking about you. I… I had to see you."

Staring at my empty wine glass and wishing it would refill, I nodded. He was saying everything I wanted to hear, but made it sound like goodbye. Why did he call me? Why was he screwing with my emotions like this?

"Are you… Is this goodbye?" I asked.

His body tensed beside me. "What? No. Not at all. I'm trying to explain why I can't let you go. I should, damnit. My being with you puts you in danger, but I'm too goddamn selfish to leave you alone. I know you need more than my silence, so I'm tryin' to lay this shit out and hope it doesn't scare you off. But you deserve to know what you're getting into."

I got it. Dominico lived a dangerous life. He couldn't promise me tomorrow, or even the next hour. I should be upset about that, and want more stability and safety, but I didn't care. Whatever this thing was between us, I wanted to explore it. Relieved he wasn't dumping me, my brain was entirely too jumbled to answer him with words, so I leaned in and kissed his lips.

He seemed startled at first, then Dominico shifted, pulling me onto his lap and deepening the kiss. A little voice in the back of my mind screamed at me that we were alone and this thing between us had the potential to go further than I'd ever gone with a guy, but I didn't care. I needed him as much as he needed me. In his arms, I wasn't worried about college bills, or Papa's depression, or restaurant stress... There was danger and fire, and strangely enough, it felt almost like floating.

We made out until the pizza came, then we broke apart long enough to eat and drink more. The conversation was easy and flirty, like it had been during our last date, and by the time I changed into my swimsuit, something big had changed between us.

"You look... wow," he said, eyeballing me as I emerged from the bathroom.

The swim trunks he wore rode low on his hips, drawing all my attention to his sculpted abs. Maybe it was the wine, but I had the sudden, foreign urge to run my fingers—and possibly my tongue—all over his stomach. My entire body heated at the thought.

"Thanks, you too."

"I mean it, Net. You have no idea how gorgeous you are."

"Net, huh?" I paused midstep, thrown off by the nickname.

He grinned and leaned forward and ducked down until we were almost nose to nose. "Yep. It's fitting. You're definitely ensnaring."

He'd gone and given me a sweet nickname, making me feel even more warm and fuzzy inside. I needed to combat these feels with a witty retort, but before I could form one, he spun around and headed outside.

I followed him into the hot tub and leaned against the side. Stars lit up the Vegas sky, and a slight breeze chilled my exposed skin. I sank deeper into the hot water and let the jets massage my sore muscles. Everything felt so wonderful. Closing my eyes, I leaned my head back against a head rest. Despite the wine, the heat, and the jets, I was far from relaxed. My entire body felt charged, alert, and acutely aware of the proximity of Dominico's shirtless body.

Opening my eyes, I checked him out again. His shoulders were broad, and the muscles of his arms and chest were as defined as his abs. He slid closer to me until our legs and arms were touching, and I continued my visual investigation of his body.

A thick scar ran down the side of his left pec and another one circled his forearm. Feeling way more brazen than I ever had in my life, I reached out and traced the one on his forearm before letting my fingertips trail up to his pec. His body shivered beneath my touch.

"Sorry," I said, pulling away.

He grabbed my hand. "Don't be. I like it when you touch me. You can touch me anywhere you want."

A loaded invitation if I'd ever heard one. My fingertips went back to their exploration of his pecs and my gaze drifted to the water bubbling against the middle of his stomach. Wanting to touch him with so much more than my fingers, I licked my lips.

Dominico wrapped his arms around me so fast my hand was trapped between our chests. Firm, demanding lips found mine, effectively capturing me as his tongue explored my mouth. He tasted like beer and desire, and as I melded my body against his he pulled me closer. Pressed hard against him, I still wasn't close enough. I wanted more of him all over me.

My hands drifted down his sculpted sides and abs. A strangled moan escaped from his lips before he pulled me from the hot tub and toweled me off. I wanted to return the favor, but he picked me up and carried me into the house. He laid a blanket on the rug in front of the fireplace and pressed the button to start the flames. Then he sat me down on the floor in front of him and brushed my hair over my shoulder so he could trail kisses down my neck.

"Can I take this off?" he asked, hooking a finger under my bikini strap.

Nervous but wanting to be naked with him, I nodded.

He tugged the tie free and released my breasts. Leaning back, he looked me over. Feeling exposed, I reached for the corner of the blanket, but he grabbed my wrist.

"No. Don't cover up. You're gorgeous."

Releasing my wrist, his hand traveled up my arm to my breasts. He shifted to his knees, freeing up both his hands to explore. I leaned back on my arms, giving him complete access. Soft, gentle caresses evolved into kneading and squeezing. Then his hands were replaced with his lips. Flames ignited in my core. Wanting to explore his body as well, I balanced on one arm and tugged on the waistband of his shorts.

He chuckled. "These in your way?"

I nodded. "Please take them off."

He slid them over his hips, and his cock sprang free. The sight stirred both desire and fear within me. I'd never been a chicken, though, so I trailed my hands down his stomach and wrapped them around his shaft. He moaned, so I gave him a little squeeze.

"Net," he breathed out, nibbling at my neck. "I want to fuck you so bad right now."

The desperation in his voice was both thrilling and terrifying. Releasing him, I laid on my back and let him tug off my bikini bottoms.

"You're so fucking beautiful," he said, staring down at me as he slid them over my feet.

Then he trailed kisses up my calf, between my knees, all the way to my inner thigh. I stilled as his lips drifted over my core and ghosted kisses and hot breath from thigh to thigh, effectively teasing me with a whisper of what was to come. I wanted more—wanted him—fisting the blanket, I tried to get myself under control. He chuckled and grabbed my thighs, spreading them wide. His tongue teased my clit, flicking it back and forth, before plunging into my pussy. Ohmigod. Overwhelmed with the sensation, I had no idea what to do. Thankfully, Dominico did. He licked and sucked on me while his hands roamed up to squeeze my breasts and pinch my nipples, intensifying my pleasure with every second. The sensation of it all drove me to the edge of bliss, but right as I was about to find release, his mouth disappeared. I heard the rip of a package, and then the next thing I knew, the throbbing head of his penis was nudging my folds.

He pushed his upper body away and looked me over again, his eyes dark and hungry, before slowly sliding into me.

My god, the size of him… it hurt. I cried out and he stilled, brushing kisses all over my neck. Still inside of me, his hot kisses moved to my lips. We made out as he reached down and fingered my clit, pleasuring me through the pain as he started moving again. Slowly, he slid in and out of me, each stroke feeling better than the last. He released my lips to suck on a nipple. Nibbling at and teasing my breasts, he continued to stroke my clit until a wave of pleasure swept away the last of the pain.

I could tell he was holding back, but I didn't need him to anymore. Ready for the rest of him, I angled my hips to give him full access.

"You okay?" he asked, his eyes locked on mine.

In answer, I kissed his neck and squeezed him inside of me.

He groaned. "You feel so fuckin' amazing," he said, plunging deeper inside me, sparking more pain, but also more pleasure. He kept his pace slow, burying himself inside of me and withdrawing, over and over. Sweat beaded across his forehead and collarbone as he gritted his teeth. He was still holding back. The pain faded again, and pleasure continued to intensify with each controlled stroke. Taking my hands in his, he held them above my head and continued to fuck me. The feeling of being contained—of being held down—only increased the fire within me. Desperate for more, I wrapped my legs around him.

"You better stop it," he said in a low growl. "You're gonna make me lose control."

That sounded fun. "Good," I said, grinding my hips against him and squeezing his dick in my pussy again.

Still holding down my hands, he fucked me harder, faster.

"You like that?" he asked. "That what you want?"

Release was so close I couldn't talk. I nodded.

"Not yet," he said, pulling out of me.

"What? Why?" I asked. My body practically thrummed with need for him to finish what he'd started.

"Because I want more. I want you every way I can take you."

Before I could respond, he kissed me, capturing my lips until I was breathless. Then he tugged my hands up, lying back, and pulling me on top of him.

"Ride me."

Slightly nervous and not entirely sure what to do, I kneeled on either side of his hips and took his length inside me while Dominico watched, his eyes heavy with lust. He moaned, and bucked, driving himself deeper inside me. Up and down his shaft I slid, encouraged by his reaction I rocked my hips back and forth. His hands squeezed my breasts and pinched my nipples while I rode him, building momentum and once again stoking the fire within me. Harder. Faster. When I was about to come, he gripped my hips and held me still as he pulled out of me.

"Not yet," he said.

I growled, and he chuckled as he sat up and wrapped his arms around me.

My body quivered as I began to come down again. He stood, pulling me up beside him. He kissed my cheek, my neck, and finally my lips, slow and soft, while I tried to keep myself from jumping on him and making him finish me off.

Releasing my lips, he whispered, "I like you like this," against my cheek. "All horny and shit. Now you finally want me as bad as I want you every time I see you. Want me to let you come?"

"What do you think?" I asked.

He pulled me back to the floor and positioned me on my hands and knees. Gripping my hips, he entered me from behind. There was nothing slow or controlled about it when Dominico finally let go. He pounded my pussy, sending waves of pleasure and pain throughout my body. Then his fingers found my clit again, stroking and circling, rocketing me into a blinding orgasm. He came with me, and then released me to collapse onto the blanket in blissful exhaustion. Dominico laid beside me and wrapped me in his arms.

"Stay with me tonight," he whispered, nuzzling my neck.

I couldn't move, let alone get home, in this condition. Eyes still closed, I nodded. He might not be able to promise me tomorrow, but tonight had been perfect.

CHAPTER FIFTEEN
Dominico

I WATCHED ANNETTA sleep, beating myself up for being so fucking weak I'd broken down and called her. My older, more responsible brother was currently out on a date with Zeta Caruso, like the good little capo's son he was, while I lie beside the girl I should have been strong enough to stay away from.

Annetta stirred, shifting the blanket I'd covered us with, to reveal her left breast. My body responded, instantly hardening with need. I thought fucking her would get her out of my system, but it had backfired. Now I just wanted her more.

Before last night, she'd been a virgin. I hadn't even considered that complication until I saw the blood. How the hell did someone as gorgeous as Annetta reach her 20's with her cherry intact? And why the fuck had she been so willing to give it to me? She said she knew what I did, so she had to know my life belonged to my family.

My thoughts drifted to Gino, who had willingly given up his life to serve the family. A guy like Gino, coming from an upright family in the sticks, couldn't have understood the price he would pay. Now he did, though. Carlo had set him up with a wife and told Gino to get her pregnant so the Durantes would have something on him to keep him in line.

"I had no strings. He wanted to tie me down with baggage... give me somethin' to lose if I turned out to be a snitch or a mole," Gino said.

Which was beyond screwed up since Gino was a mole. I stared at him, wondering what to say.

"She's pregnant with our second kid... another boy. We're naming him Franco after my grandfather. The oldest is Antonio. We call him Tony. He just turned two, and he's a handful." Gino chuckled. *"Cutest little asshole you ever saw. I know I'm not supposed to get attached to them, but they're innocent in all this, you know? I didn't think it would be like this, but I can't help but feel responsible for them."*

A year older than me with a wife and two kids I hadn't known a damn thing about. How the hell was it possible? I nodded, still too shocked to form a reply.

"It's not like I love her or anything," he hurried to defend himself. *"But she's a good woman, and she doesn't know anything about this... about what I'm doing. If this goes south, and I... Will you keep an eye on them?"*

He didn't have to be here. He'd given everything to come work for my family and now he needed me to protect his if he got caught by the Durantes. There was only one answer I could give him. *"Yeah, of course."*

He sighed, his shoulders instantly relaxing. *"Thank you, Dom. You won't be able to help them directly, because she can't ever know who I really am. It'll put them all in danger. But... whatever you can do."*

I clapped a hand on his shoulder. *"I get it, man. I'll make sure they're okay."*

"Thanks again. You don't know what this means to me."

"You don't love her?"

I don't know why I couldn't get past his confession. Maybe because I wanted to believe I could force some sort of feeling into an arranged marriage.

Gino's eyebrows rose. "I'm a family man, Dom. It's business. You don't get too close, you know?"

Yeah, I did know, which is why I swore off Annetta Porro that night, knowing the more time I spent with her the harder it would be to marry Valentina. I locked down my feelings and vowed to do my duty like Gino had. Like Michael was. Family had to come first. If Gino could live that way, so could I. I was determined.

I barely lasted three weeks before calling her. If she hadn't agreed to come with me, I might have broken down her door and kidnapped her. And as she slept naked beside me, I realized just how screwed I was.

Her perfect body, soft and firm in all the right places, called to my hands to touch it. I traced a finger over her exposed breast, up her neck, and to her plump, slightly parted lips. She opened her eyes slowly, and inviting jade pools gazed up at me. "Hey," she said, her voice husky with sleep.

"Mornin,' Net." The girl had me all tangled and tripped up. I didn't know what to do about her, but I was sure as hell enjoying being caught. "Don't sleep. I don't know how long I'll get to keep you."

She knuckled her eyes. "What do you want to do, then?"

My gaze drifted down her body. I had a few ideas, but wanted more than sex from her. I wanted… everything. "Talk to me. Tell me more about yourself."

"Like what?"

"Anything. Everything. What's your favorite color? Favorite movie? Favorite food? Whatever shit pops into your mind," I said.

"Okay." She tugged the blanket up over her exposed breast and I stopped her.

"Please?" I asked. "I want to see you, too."

She released the blanket and I wrapped my arm around her stomach, feeling the curves of her hips.

"So who's the guy in the Celica?" I asked, still hung up on what her old man had said.

"Crap, I was supposed to call him last night."

The idea of Annetta calling another man pissed me off. Struggling not to show how badly I wanted to find this guy and rip out his throat, I asked. "Why? Who is he?"

"Just a friend I work with," she said, but there was something more in her voice.

Looking into her eyes, I asked, "Just a friend?"

She nodded. "I think he wants more, but I... I want this. I want you."

I knew she was telling the truth, but hearing that some bastard was making a play for her made me feel the need to claim her again. In fact, I wanted to lock her up and never let the asshole so much as see her again.

"He can't have more," I said, nuzzling her neck. My hand drifted down between her thighs to get her ready for me. "You're mine now."

Her breath caught as I circled her clit. Regaining her composure, she stared me down and asked, "Really? When did I agree to that?"

I wanted her again. Kissing her sassy lips, I slid a finger inside her. She was already wet. I slid my finger deeper, and when she moaned, added a second and stroked her g-spot.

"Right now," I said against her lips, still staring into her eyes. "Tell me you're mine."

She moaned again, grinding her soaking pussy against my fingers. I slid them out, climbed on top of her, and pinned her beneath my body, the head of my dick waiting at her entrance. She tried to grind against me, but I held her still.

"No. Not until you tell me you're mine, Net. I need to hear the words."

"I'm here with you," she whispered.

"Not good enough. I won't share you. I'll kill anyone stupid enough to touch you. You're mine."

"Of course I'm yours," she said. "Think I'd do what we did last night with just anyone?"

"You better not." I nibbled her neck, barely able to contain myself. "You make me so goddamn crazy. I just... I need to feel you. I don't want to use a condom this time."

"I'm on the pill," she said.

Taking her announcement as permission, I started to slide into her, but she stopped me.

"I won't share you, either, Dom. You're mine, too."

Fierce, beautiful, so damn sexy I couldn't hold back anymore. I slid deep inside her, and she felt so amazing I almost came right then. I stilled, fighting for control. "This is mine. All mine."

I drove into her again and her lips parted with a moan. I thought about shoving my dick in her mouth, but knew I wouldn't last. Instead, I popped a perfect pink nipple in my mouth and sucked, grazing it with my teeth. Annetta squeezed me inside her and I almost lost my shit.

"You're gonna make me come," I warned.

"Good," she breathed. "Fuck me."

I never knew that word could be so sexy. Her eyes were closed. I set my hands on either side of her face and said, "Look at me."

Her eyelids fluttered open and bright green eyes watched me as I plunged into her again and again.

"Say my name," I said. "And tell me what you want me to do to you again."

She was panting. We both were.

"Fuck me, Dom," she said.

Barely hanging on, I thrust into her again. Harder. Again. Her body writhed beneath me, angling to get me in the perfect spot. Once I hit it, she began to unravel. Faster. Her eyes drifted closed as she called out my name again. One last thrust, and I was done. Breathing hard, I collapsed on top of her and kissed her neck.

I got up to hit the bathroom about an hour later, accidentally waking Annetta in the process. When I finished, we snuggled in front of the fireplace, alternating between talking, laughing, and messing around until the sun came up.

All too early, my pager went off - reality calling me to return. I phoned in and confirmed that Carlo needed me to do a couple of pickups. Annetta and I put the blankets we'd used in the dirty clothes hamper and locked up the house.

The drive to Annetta's was quiet, and I got the sense she was no readier to go home than I was to drop her off. Still, duty called, so I walked her to the door.

"I don't know when I'll be able to see you again," I said.

"I get it," she replied, searching my face. "But try to call every once in a while, and let me know you're okay. I worry about you."

She was so damn sweet, I wanted to wrap her in my arms and shield her from my shitty world. "Don't let the Celica guy touch you," I said. She hadn't mentioned her friend's name, but I knew where he worked and what he drove. I'd have it by the end of the day.

She rolled her eyes. "I'm not a slut, Dom. You have nothing to worry about."

Trapping her between my body and the door, I gave her one last kiss before letting her into the house. Then, I went back to work.

* * *

The rest of the week passed in a blur of business as usual. Saturday evening I worked another of Carlo's poker games before helping Michael intercept a forty-foot truck of liquor bound for the Columbian. Successful heists that broke up the Durante's supply chain always put my old man in a good mood. He slapped me and Michael on our backs and broke out the good cigars. Then he let us know that Mom and Mrs. Caruso were planning Michael and Zeta's engagement party.

Knowing I'd be next, and practically hearing the clock tick against my time as a bachelor, I tried to get away to see Annetta, but the old man kept me tied up. With the hits on our warehouses, we were short staffed, so Father had me and Michael making rounds to pick up and drop money. He didn't want us flying solo and he sure as hell didn't want us off doing our own thing. Michael was practically glued to my hip, making it almost impossible to call my girl, much less go see her.

My first chance to break away came Tuesday night when Michael was roped into having dinner with his future in-laws. It only took a quick phone call to the restaurant to find out when Annetta's shift ended and to get the name of the Celica driver: Brandon Smith. I dropped by the Davenport Hotel to call in a favor with their desk clerk, who would book me a room on cash, before hauling ass back to the restaurant. Arriving only minutes before Annetta's shift let out, I lit up a smoke by the back door and waited.

A man emerged, took one look at me, and then leaned against the wall. He had dishwater blond hair, average height, average build, and looked exactly like Collin's description.

"You Brandon?" I asked.

He eyed me. "Yeah. Do I know you?"

I took a final deep drag before dropping my cigarette and crushing it under my steel-toed shoe. "No, but I wanted to thank you for giving my girl a lift to and from work. It's uh... nice of you to take an interest in her safety like that."

His brow furrowed. "Your girl?" He looked at the door. "Annetta's... your girl?"

She hadn't told him about me, huh? Wondering why, but trying not to let it bug me, I nodded. "Yeah. In fact, I'm picking her up tonight, so you can go ahead and head home."

He continued to watch me, making no move to leave.

Who the fuck did this guy think he was? "You got a hearing problem?" I asked.

"No." He frowned. "I'll just wait and make sure that's cool with Annetta."

As I was mentally ripping Brandon's arms from his body, Annetta emerged from the restaurant. She paused, midstep, and smiled at me, her eyes bright.

"Dom!" Leaving the door wide open behind her, she lunged, sliding her arms under my jacket to hug me.

All concerns I'd had about her and Brandon-the-asshole disappeared as I breathed her in and gave her a peck on the lips before releasing her. Keeping an arm wrapped around her waist, I dismissed Brandon. "See, we're good."

"I'll catch you tomorrow Annetta," he said, pushing off the building and heading for his car.

Annetta frowned, looking from me to Brandon. "Okay. I'll see you tomorrow." Then to me, she asked, "What did you say to him?"

I pasted on my best innocent face, acting like I hadn't been ready to kill him. "Nothing. I was just sizing up the competition."

She rolled her eyes. "You're ridiculous. I told you, there is no competition."

Music to my ears. I grabbed her arms and pulled her in for a longer kiss, knowing full well I shouldn't be doing it in the parking lot of a restaurant under my family's protection. Anyone could see us, and if word got back to my old man or the Pelinos, all hell would break loose. But Annetta was like a drug that I couldn't get enough of. Knowing she'd probably get me killed only made me want to take more of her in. Hair pulled back in a bun, smelling of pasta sauce, I'd never seen a more beautiful sight. I wanted to fuck her in the parking lot. Barely controlling myself, I released her and led her to my Porsche.

"Thanks for picking me up," she said.

"I couldn't stay away." My hand rested high on her thigh. It had been almost a week since I'd spent the night with her, and it was all I could do not to lay her chair back and rip her clothes off. "I need you, Net."

Her breath caught. "I missed you. Where are we going?" She buckled up.

"Another surprise."

I drove us to the hotel I'd visited earlier, grabbed my bag from the back, and let us in the side door using the keycard I'd picked up from the desk clerk earlier.

"What are we doing here?" Annetta asked as I led her to the elevator.

"Going to our room."

"Our room?" Her eyebrows rose. "Do you have a permanent room here?"

Wondering what she was asking, I stared at her.

"That you bring all your girls to?"

I laughed. I couldn't help it. She was jealous and gorgeous and my god, I wanted to fuck her right there in the elevator.

"What?" she asked. "It's a valid question."

"No… it's not," I said, taking a deep breath to get my laughter under control. "You must think I have way more time on my hands than I actually do. Trust me, Net, if I had the time, I would have a permanent hotel room, but you'd be tied up in there waiting for me."

Her eyes widened.

I pulled her into me, capturing those beautiful, full lips while my hands slid down to grab her ass. The elevator doors dinged open and she pulled away. Keeping hold of her hand, I found our room and let us in.

Although small and conservative compared to the suites in my father's casino, the room was also clean and bright. A king bed filled the wall to the right with a small kitchenette and bathroom to the left. The best part about it, however, was the oversized jetted tub positioned in front of the giant windows.

"This is nice," Annetta said, drifting away from me to look around, her gaze landing on the bottle of champagne, chocolates, and flowers on the bar. Beaming a smile at me, she asked, "What's all this?"

"An apology for staying away so long."

"You don't have to apologize, Dom." She picked up the bottle of champagne and examined it. "I know you're busy."

She was so goddamn perfect. I closed the distance between us, wrapped her in my arms, and started nibbling on her neck.

Giggling, she pushed me away. "Shower first. I smell like the restaurant."

I undid the top button of her blouse. "No shower, bathtub." I led her to it and turned on the water.

Her gaze drifted from me to the tub. "But I didn't bring a swimsuit."

"Think I'd let you wear one?"

I unbuttoned the rest of her blouse and slid it from her shoulders. Her lacy pink bra was the next thing to go. It fell to the floor, exposing her perfect breasts, nipples already dark, erect, and begging for me to suck on them.

"How's that water coming?" she asked, sounding adorably nervous.

Glancing over my shoulder to check on the tub, I said, "Like we need to get you naked."

With one swift motion, I tugged her elastic wasted chef pants down to her ankles. Her panties matched her bra. I pulled her to me and turned her away, so her ass was pressed against my now hard dick. Kissing her bare shoulders, one of my hands played with her breasts while the other dipped down over her stomach to rub the silky lace of her panties against her clit.

She was already wet. I spent some time enjoying the feel of her wet panties before pushing them aside and dipping two fingers into her pussy. She moaned and adjusted her hips, giving me better access. My fingers played inside her as I memorized her body's reactions, paying close attention to what made her moan the loudest. I loved pleasing her like this, and before too long, I focused on her g-spot, and really went to town. Annetta's breathing grew shallow and labored as I plunged my fingers into her harder and faster until she released around me.

When she was done, I helped her into the tub, undressed, and climbed in beside her, standing. Her gaze lingered on my dick.

"See something you like?" I asked.

She blushed. "I wanna try… something."

The possibilities only made me harder. "We can try anything you want, Net."

She reached up and grabbed my dick, giving it a little squeeze. I moaned. She smiled and started stroking me. "You like that?" she asked.

I nodded.

She tugged me closer to her and slid me inside her mouth. I've had blow jobs before, but something about Annetta's plump lips wrapped around my dick made me lose my mind. As she sucked and teased me, I grabbed the back of her head and pulled her further up my shaft. Remembering she'd been a virgin before our last encounter and fearing I might have gone too far, I watched her for a sign of how she felt about this. When she looked up at me with a grin tugging at her lips and a mischievous sparkle in her eyes, god dammit, I think I fell in love.

I fucked her mouth as her hands wrapped around me and squeezed my ass. I let her take me to the brink, and then released her head and pulled out.

"Fuck," I breathed.

Sparkle still dancing in her eyes, grin still tugging at her lips, she said, "You like that?"

In answer, I climbed on top of her and buried myself deep in her pussy.

She gasped.

"You like that?" I asked, turning her own question on her.

"Yes. Fuck me, Dom."

One thing was certain, she wasn't a virgin anymore. I made her come, and then pulled her out of the tub. With my fingers inside her and her hand stroking my dick, we each drained a glass of champagne. Then I talked her into letting me pour it on her and lick it off. She returned the favor, and we ended up back in the tub.

By the time I dropped her off at home the next morning, the sheets were full of champagne and all the towels had been used.

CHAPTER SIXTEEN
Dominico

*O*VER THE NEXT several weeks, Annetta and I kept up our secret relationship. Whenever I could get away, we'd slip off to the Davenport Hotel, room 325, and fuck until morning. I knew I was playing a dangerous game, but I couldn't force myself to quit her.

In August, Abriana married and moved to California with Romario De Lucca. I called her a couple of times, and although she didn't sound happy, she was alive and healthy, which I told myself had to be enough. The attacks on the family increased, and the De Luccas had given us the leg up, steadily supplying weapon shipments and helping us organize strikes against the Durantes.

The Commission was still trying to place a messaggero, and my father's paranoia kept increasing at an alarming rate. He had every available wiseguy working around the clock. With lengthened workdays, and Father demanding more of my time, my free-time with Annetta was basically non-existent.

September brought on Michael's engagement dinner. Since the Carusos hosted, we didn't return to Annetta's restaurant. Which was a good thing, since Valentina was at the party and wouldn't shut up about me and her getting hitched. With Valentina's eighteenth birthday less than six months away, my future looked bleak. As the goddamn pink-lipped octopus butted her shrill voice and immature opinions into my dinner conversation with Mario, I lost my appetite. Tossing my napkin onto my untouched plate, I escaped the stuffy banquet hall and headed outside for air.

That bitch was gonna be my wife.

I couldn't begin to come to grips with it. Not after Annetta. Thoughts of my girl's perfect lips and bright green eyes churned my stomach even more. I would have to tell her about Valentina soon. Then what? I couldn't let her go.

Would Annetta agree to be my mistress?

The thought made me laugh. My feisty little firecracker would likely stab me rather than sleep with me after she found out I'd have to marry someone else.

Maybe Annetta and I could disappear...

My head was in a very dark place when Mamma found me.

"What is wrong?" she asked, joining me at the porch railing.

No sense in worrying her with something she couldn't do anything about. "Nothing," I lied. "I'm just tired."

"Don't you lie to your mamma, *mio figlio,*" she tsked, frowning as she studied my face. "And don't pretend I can't see the truth for myself. *Avere un chiodo fisso in testa.*"

The old saying—an accusation that I had a nail fixed in my head—was the Italian way of saying I had a bee in my bonnet. I couldn't help but chuckle at her idiom. "It's not a nail, Mamma. More like being caught in a net." Realizing I shouldn't have even said that much, I clamped my mouth shut.

Her forehead scrunched up. "And you think you can get away with that little of an explanation?" she asked. "No. You tell me what is wrong right this instant."

I tried to shrug her off again. "Leave it be. You can't fix it."

That was apparently the wrong thing to say, because her eyes flashed with anger. She glared from me to the door leading back to the dinner.

"Don't you talk to me like that, Dominico. Your father may have forgotten who I am, but I haven't. I may not have been born the son my father wanted, but I am far from the helpless girl he thought I was. You would all be wise to remember that and not underestimate me."

I'd never seen Mamma so pissed before. Somebody must have set her off. Lowering my gaze, I apologized. She patted my cheek and demanded again that I tell her what was wrong.

"Just a girl."

A smile softened her features, smoothing away some of her previous anger. "It's always a girl, my boy. I take it Valentina Pelino isn't the girl who has you sulking outside your brother's engagement dinner."

"I'm not sulking and I... It doesn't matter."

Her eyes narrowed. "Why don't you tell me what's going on, and I'll decide whether or not it matters."

Against my better judgment, I broke down and told Mamma all about Annetta. I'd planned to make it sound like a meaningless fling, but once I started talking, I couldn't stop.

Mamma waited for me to finish before frowning. "It's worse than I thought."

Stunned, I stared at her. "You knew about her?"

"Of course I do, dear."

"But—" Shit. If Mamma knew about Annetta, then Father must...

"I know everything that happens in this city, Dom," Mamma said. "And I let your father in on only what he needs to know."

Sometimes I felt like I didn't know Mamma at all.

"I knew you were sneaking off to be with her, but I didn't realize it had gone this far. What is she to you."

"She's…" How could I even answer that? "I love her, Mamma. I know it doesn't matter, because of the Pelinos, but I do." Admitting it aloud didn't change anything, but it did make me feel better.

"Her family has loose connections on the east coast, but they were never involved."

And how had Mamma found that out? We'd done a thorough check before hiring her at the restaurant and hadn't found anything.

"Her father owes some money to Don Rocchi… loans he took out for Annetta's schooling."

Another fact I knew nothing about.

"Well, what's she made of? Think she can handle all this?"

Did I? "I don't know, but she's strong like you. She hasn't freaked out about my absences or tried to manipulate me into anything."

Mamma sighed and pulled me down into a hug, rubbing my back like I was five years old with a scraped knee again. "Let me think about this," she said. "Don't do anything crazy."

I chuckled at the idea, wondering what she thought either of us could do. No matter who Mamma had been and how much information she had, it was suicide to go against my father. Especially with his growing paranoia.

"Yes, Mamma," I said to appease her.

She kissed my cheeks and sent me back inside to do my old man's bidding.

*   *   *

The next day, Michael and I were trailing one of our delivery vehicles when it got hit. We'd stayed a few cars behind, trying to stay out of sight, and were caught behind a light. When the light changed, Michael sped up to catch the van, weaving in and out of vehicles. Michael was still speeding when I spotted the van parked in a vacant lot, partially blocked a black SUV.

"There!" I shouted, pointing it out.

As I was craning my neck around to see what the hell was going on, Michael turned a hard right, jumping the curb and barely missing a fence before coming to a screeching stop beside the SUV.

My pistol was in my hand before I opened the door and lurched out of the car.

Two suppressed shots rang out.

With Michael by my side, I rushed to the SUV, grabbed my knife, and slashed the front driver's side tire. No matter what happened, these bastards wouldn't be able to make a clean getaway. Michael and I circled the SUV, him at the back, me at the front, and I came face to face with the business end of a pistol.

"Drop your fuckin' weapon," the wielder growled.

"Fuck you," Michael said. "You drop your fuckin' weapons."

There were four of us. Everyone had guns drawn. I'd heard stories from old mobsters about shootouts like this. Someone always died, usually the guy who shot first, but always the man who didn't fire at all. My heart pounded so hard I wouldn't be surprised if everyone could hear it over the traffic on the other side of the vehicles. I watched the guy in front of me, waiting for the slightest indication that he was about to pull the trigger.

"Everyone calm down," Michael said, using his "boss" voice. "Let's fix this so we all get out alive."

No way in hell was that happening. These bastards had just hit one of our deliveries. If we didn't bring them in or kill them, Father would kill us. But sure, I could pretend to play nice if it meant not getting my brains blown out in some goddamn parking lot.

Two more suppressed shots.

Before I could squeeze the trigger, the guy in front of me toppled. On the way down, he fired a wild shot that grazed my right forearm before puncturing the side of the SUV.

I grabbed my bleeding arm with my left hand and shot the asshole again to make sure he was good and dead. When I looked up, Michael was running to our delivery van. I followed him to find a soldier by the name of Rocco slumped over the passenger's seat, pistol still in his left hand while he held his bleeding stomach with the right.

"I got the bastard," Rocco whispered.

Then he leaned back, closed his eyes, and died.

Shit. "What do we do?" I asked Michael.

We couldn't leave the bodies there. If, by some miracle of a chance, nobody had called in the shots, some cop would eventually drive by to investigate the nice, newer-looking vehicles parked in an abandoned lot, and we'd be screwed.

Gesturing to my arm, Michael said, "Wrap that shit up and help me load the bodies."

Once we got all four bodies loaded in the back of the van, Michael told me to drive it to the drop point.

"You've got to be kidding," I said, wiping blood off my hands onto a rag. "Why me?"

He leveled a hard stare at me. "Because I said."

It was the "boss" voice again. He'd never used it on me before. Stunned, I stared back at him, waiting for him to claim it was a joke or something, but my brother's expression didn't crack. If anything, it hardened.

"That's it then?" I asked, still disbelieving my ears and eyes. "You're pullin' rank? We don't even get to rock, paper, scissors for the shit jobs anymore?"

He turned his back on me, heading for his Acura. "I'll meet you there."

"Fuck you," I shouted to his back, hurt and angry that my brother would treat me like hired help. Michael could be an asshole, but he usually wasn't a condescending prick. At least, not to me. Wanting to flick more shit at him, I said the one thing I knew he'd hate. "Congratulations, Mikey, you're turning out just like the old man."

"Go to hell, Dom," he said before disappearing around the SUV.

Shaking my head, I climbed into the van full of four dead bodies and a shit-ton of drugs. Knowing that if I got pulled over I was done for, I made myself take a couple deep breaths before turning over the engine and driving the speed limit to the drop point.

A half hour later, with the van tucked safely inside one of our warehouses, there was no way in hell I was getting back in Michael's car. Still fuming, I walked to the payphone down the street and called Mario to pick me up. Then, because I was angry and coming down from a near-death experience, I dialed Annetta, hoping she'd make everything better. Not quite.

"Thank god you called," she said with an urgency that immediately put me back on alert.

"What's wrong?" I asked.

"I... I can't talk to you over the phone about this, Dom. I need to see you."

We'd been together for months, and I'd never heard her sound so desperate and afraid. My mind raced at the possibilities. Had someone found out about us and threatened her? Or had she finally come to her senses enough to brush me off for good? Both options twisted my stomach in knots.

"I don't know if I can get away tonight."

"Please, Dom. I really need to talk to you."

Shit. Trying to figure out what to do, I said, "I'll be there."

"Soon?" she asked. "It's important."

I leaned against the phone booth. "Yeah. Soon. I promise."

She sighed heavily. "Thank you. I'll see you soon."

I disconnected and waited for Mario, wondering what could be so damn important that Annetta needed to see me "soon." I thought about calling Mario back and telling him I'd grab a cab instead, but he'd most likely already left. Besides, most of the city's cabbies were in the pocket of one family or another. Either they'd report back to my old man, or I'd lead my enemies to Annetta's doorstep.

With the cab out of the question, I planned to have Mario drop me off at the casino to grab my car, but by the time he arrived I was a mess. I needed to know what was wrong with Annetta. And if I couldn't trust my best friend, who could I trust?

"Hey," I said, climbing into the passenger's seat. "I need you to take me to Annetta's, but you gotta keep it between us, okay?"

He stared at me, his brow furrowed. I was afraid he'd ask questions that would put him in danger, but instead, he nodded. "Okay, Dom. Whatever you need."

Grateful, I laid back and watched the blocks roll by. I'd just survived a life and death situation, drove a van loaded with bodies and drugs, and neither of those held a candle to the fear I felt as we approached Annetta's house. Had she found out that I was stuck with Valentina? Was she dumping me? I couldn't handle the thought of never touching her… never hearing her laugh… never seeing those brilliant green eyes… never being inside of her… again.

Mario parked in front of her house. Her father's truck was gone and the place was quiet. I pounded on the door. No answer. Worried, I pounded again. When it swung open, I was staring at someone who wasn't Annetta.

"Where's Net?" I asked.

The girl eyed me up and down like she could take me before saying, "You must be Dom. You better do right by my girl, or you're gonna have to deal with me, I don't care who the fuck you are."

She weighed maybe a buck twenty-five, and I wasn't scared. Still, I couldn't help but wonder what she meant. When hadn't I done right by Annetta? Had I done something to hurt her?

"Okay, where is she?" I asked.

"In her room," she waved in the direction. "Now I'm gonna go have a little talk with your boy Mario and remind him why he needs to call regularly." She walked past me, leaving the door open.

I found Annetta sitting on a bed in what I could only assume was her room. She wore shorts and a T-shirt, and her eyes were red, like she'd been crying.

"What's wrong?" I asked.

"Come in," she said, waving me forward. "Have a seat. I'll be right back."

Like I could sit without knowing what had her so upset. I stood in the doorway, looking around her room. It looked different from my sister's bedroom. Yes, Annetta's walls were pink, but there were no magazine pictures of boy bands plastered across the walls, no clothes hanging everywhere, no vanity filled with makeup and shit. All Annetta had in her room was a dresser with a mirror, a bed, and a bookshelf full of paperbacks. I walked over and read the cover to one. Mystery.

Interesting. I didn't know she was into mysteries. I must have scored a buttload of points by taking her to the escape room. So why was she so upset now? Before I could investigate further, Annetta returned carrying some sort of white stick. My stomach plummeted as she held it between us.

"What is that?" I asked, even though a part of me already knew.

"A pregnancy test. It's positive. I'm… I'm pregnant."

I looked from the stick to her face, and then back to the stick. "Are you sure? I thought you were on the pill."

She nodded. "I checked twice, and the clinic confirmed it."

Okay, now I needed to sit down. My legs shuffled until I felt the bed behind me. I collapsed. "How far along?"

Annetta stayed where she stood. "Almost four months."

"Four months?" I asked. "Why didn't you tell me sooner?"

"I didn't know. I didn't get morning sickness. But last week at work the smell of chicken cooking made me…" She swallowed. "It was bad. Then I realized I hadn't had my period in... a while. Adona bought me a couple of tests, and here we are."

I shook my head, unable to make sense of it. Although I shouldn't be surprised, since we didn't always use protection, I still was. She was having a baby. My baby. I was going to be a dad. The thought filled me with immeasurable pride and fear. "I don't know what to say."

She looked stricken. "I... I don't expect anything from you. I know your work is complicated and you can't... promise me tomorrow. I get that." She wrapped her hands protectively around her stomach. "But... I... I heard his heartbeat, and I can't abort him. I can do this. I know it's going to be difficult, but I can—"

"It's a boy?" I asked.

"They can't tell yet. But I've been reading a bunch of books and they say morning sickness is worse with girls and since I didn't have any... it's just a guess. A hunch."

She was rambling, and I could barely string three words together. Annetta was pregnant with my child. I wanted to shout it from the rooftops, but also hide it from the world. If my father or Don Pelino found out...

"Shit," I said, standing.

Her face whipped around like I'd slapped her. "I'm not asking for anything from you, Dom. You don't need to get angry, I'm only telling you because I thought... because I..."

She didn't understand. I closed the distance between us and wrapped her in my arms. "It's not that, Net. I need some time to process. I want to be involved, and I want to be with you, but I need to figure some things out."

She nodded against my shoulder. "Yes. I know this is a lot to lay on you. I'm sorry."

"Stop." She still didn't get it. "You have nothing to be sorry for. You're having my fuckin' baby." I couldn't suppress the smile that spread across my face. Despite all the challenges I knew we'd face, I was happy. Beyond happy.

She giggled, looking up at me through lashes still wet with tears. "You're not mad?"

"No. I love you, Net. We'll figure this out."

She released a breath, her shoulders relaxing. "Thank you."

Knowing she needed me as much as I needed her right then, I pulled her shirt over her head and unhooked her bra. Her breasts were bigger, fuller. I palmed them, noting how different they felt in my hands.

"They grew," she said, blushing.

"They're still perfect."

Next, I undid her shorts and slid them down, removing her panties at the same time. Her breath caught as my fingers stroked her clit. She threw back her head and let me play with her until I tugged her forward to join me on the bed.

"I don't know how much time we have," Annetta said, glancing at the clock on her dresser. "Papa should be home soon."

It didn't matter. She needed this. We both did. I laid her on her back and slid my pants down to my ankles, keeping the rest of my clothes on. I sucked on her clit until she was swollen and ready for me, and then I moved up her body until I got to her lips.

"I'm glad you're having my baby," I said. My hands lingered on her belly, feeling the little bump that was our child. "I love you, and I'll love him. We got this. I promise."

Trust and admiration shone in her eyes as she replied, "I love you so much."

I buried my shaft inside her. Annetta squeezed her pussy around me and I picked up my pace. I fucked her until we got the release we both desperately needed.

Afterwards, I wrapped my arms around her stomach and held them both, wondering how I was gonna make good on my promise.

CHAPTER SEVENTEEN
Annetta

THE MORNING AFTER I told Dominico about the baby, I was getting ready for work when someone knocked on the door. Papa had long since headed off to his own job, so I answered to find a beautiful woman—approximately Papa's age—standing on my doorstep. Her dress managed to look both casual and expensive, probably out of some designer's collection. Big dark curls with strands of silver framed her face, her cheekbones were high, her lips were red and plump, and intelligence shone in her dark eyes.

She studied me from head to toe before saying, "You must be Annetta. You're even more lovely than he described."

He? He who? While my brain was still forming questions, my manners kicked in. "Thank you. I—"

"Oh, I'm sorry. How thoughtless of me to not introduce myself first. I'm Rosalie Mariani, dear, Dom's mother."

I stood there like an idiot, wondering why she was on my doorstep. Dressed in my restaurant uniform with my hair pulled back in a bun, wasn't the first impression I wanted to give his wealthy mafia family. Dominico should have warned me first. Self-conscious, I reached out to offer her a handshake. "It's nice to meet you, Mrs. Mariani. I'm sorry, I wasn't expecting anyone."

Ignoring my hand, she said, "Please, call me Rosalie, dear."

Pulling back my awkward, outstretched hand I glanced at my watch. Brandon hadn't picked me up for work since he'd seen me with Dom—we'd agreed that was for the best—so I needed to be out the door in thirteen minutes to catch the bus.

"Would you like to come in?" I asked.

She remained on my doorstep. "Actually, I was hoping I could interest you in spending the day with me, so we can get to know each other a little better."

I'd told Dom I was pregnant, and now his mom stood on my doorstep. He must have sent her, but why hadn't he called me first?

"I'd love to, but I have to work soon." I gestured at my uniform. "I was just about to leave for my shift."

"I hope you don't mind, but I've already called Camellia and she assured me Collin will be able to find someone to cover for you." Pushing past me, she stepped into the living room. As she looked around, her nose wrinkled in disgust.

Annoyed at her expression and still confused, I asked. "Camellia?"

She gave me a tight, condescending smile "The owner's wife. We're old friends."

She'd called into work for me? She spoke so casually about rearranging my schedule, and ruining my perfect work attendance—without my knowledge or approval—that I wanted to scream. She hoped I didn't mind? Of course I minded. Who did this woman think she was?

"I'm sorry, you did what?" I asked.

"Don't worry, dear. You're carrying a Mariani. You don't need to work anymore. We'll take care of everything. You just worry about growing my grandchild."

Dominico had called his mother "nice," but this woman was presumptuous and arrogant. Part of me wanted to roll over and let her bash me, because I loved Dominico and didn't want to create waves, but I sure as hell wasn't going to let her bully or manipulate me into giving up the job I'd worked so hard to get.

Hiding my trembling hands behind my back, I said, "Thank you for your concern," my voice only slightly wavering. "But I enjoy my job and I can do both. Women have been working and raising babies for a long time."

She cast another dismissive glance around my living room. "If this is about you needing money, because we have resources."

Did she think I was some sort of gold digger, trapping her son with a child? Struggling to keep my tone respectful, I forced what I hoped looked like a smile. "It's not about the money, Mrs. Mariani. With all due respect, I do not want your family's money. I love Dom. He's kind and intelligent and, despite who he is, he has a good heart. I love our baby and I *will* provide for him."

"Despite who he is?" she asked, her eyes hardening.

The barb felt good, but I regretted it the second it crossed my lips. I couldn't take it back, though, and no answer I could give her would make it better. "I'm sorry. That was out of line."

She held my gaze, her tight smile turning cold and calculating. Seconds ticked by as I wondered if she was there to kill me. I didn't doubt that she could. It seriously felt like her eyeballs were trying to freeze me from the soul out. I wanted to run and hide, but didn't dare show weakness.

Finally, she melted. A real smile spread across her face and her eyes softened, taking her from beautiful to stunning. "Good, you have a backbone. You're gonna need it."

Wondering what had just happened, and whether or not I was still in mortal danger, I stared at her.

"I had to be certain," Rosalie continued. "I will not allow Dom to risk everything for some weak, pathetic girl who will no doubt get him killed."

My mind rewound our conversation. "So... you didn't change my work schedule?" I asked.

"Of course I did. I'm here to help you, dear, so we need to talk. I'm famished. Let's go get lunch."

My brain could not keep up. She'd complimented me, insulted me, offended me, possibly complimented me again, and for a few seconds there, I thought she was going to kill me with her eyes. Now she wanted to take me to lunch? The woman was giving me mental whiplash.

"Would you like to change first?" she asked, looking pointedly at my uniform.

I hadn't even decided whether I should leave with her or board myself up in my room, but real smile or not, Rosalie clearly was not the type of woman people said no to. Besides, something she'd said kept bugging me.

"Wait, what do you mean by sacrificing everything? Is Dom's life in danger?" I asked.

"Now you're asking the right questions. Go change, then we'll talk over lunch."

Wishing I could contact Dominico to make sure he was okay and to get some advice or information, I hurried to my room to change. Unmarried and pregnant with her son's child, I could guess what kind of woman she probably thought I was. Determined to make her see me and not the situation, I tugged on my most modest dress—floral and knee-length with a fitted waist—let my hair down, and checked out my reflection.

My baby bump was starting to show. My clothes had been getting tight lately, but before the pregnancy tests, I'd dismissed it as too much pasta. Still unable to believe I was going to be a mom, I rubbed my belly and said a quick prayer that I was doing the right thing by leaving my house with his scary grandmother, draped a shawl over my shoulders, and headed out.

Rosalie drove an immaculate white Lincoln Town Car with tan leather interior and powered everything.

"I thought we'd start at the spa," she said as we climbed in. "I could go for a little pampering, and I'm sure you could, too. The past few days have no doubt been stressful for you."

That was an understatement. Waiting for Dominico to call so I could tell him about our baby had just about killed me. Although he and I had spoken about many things, we'd never once discussed kids and whether or not he wanted any. I hadn't even considered the option until I suspected I was pregnant. But now that I had this little guy growing inside me, nobody was taking him away.

"Is Dom in danger?" I asked again.

"We'll get to that, dear. First tell me about yourself. I want to know all about your family, your job, anything else important to you."

And I wanted to know what was going on with the father of my child, but the important conversation would have to wait until Rosalie got her answers. Taking a deep breath, I relented, and told her everything about myself, answering questions as she fired them off. Yes, my mom had died of cancer. No, I'd never spoken to anyone from the mafia on the east coast. Yes, I enjoyed cooking. No, none of the families had planted me in the restaurant. By the time we got to the spa, I felt like I'd been through the strangest, most non-politically correct, interview of my life.

She dropped all serious conversation the moment we stepped into the spa, morphing into an average, everyday mom who was determined to be manicured, pedicured, massaged, fed, and mud bathed.

During lunch, she broke out a few stories about Dominico's childhood, all of which had me rolling with laughter. According to her, he'd been quite the clown, suspended for everything from mooning his teacher to putting fake spiders in the principal's office. He and Michael had run off more nannies than she could count.

"Those two always made me laugh," she said, her eyes misty with memories. "Of course, sometimes I had to wait until he'd left the room, but I always got a chuckle out of his antics. I miss those days."

The way she sounded like those days had come to an end made me sad. "I can't speak for Michael, but Dom makes me laugh all the time," I hurried to reassure her. "He's got a great sense of humor. It was the first thing I noticed about him."

Really, it was the second, but I wasn't about to tell her I'd first been attracted to her son's delicious body and dangerous smirk.

She studied me, as if trying to decide whether or not I was telling the truth. "Forgive me, Annetta, but it's been a long time since I've heard my son laugh. It's good to hear that he still has the ability."

Despite my first impression of her, Rosalie turned out to be a gem. Granted, she still scared the hell out of me, but I kinda wanted to be her when I grew up. As our pampering came to an end, she took me into a small room where she sat us down facing each other and held my hands in hers. Suspecting that she was finally about to divulge why Dominico was in danger, I leaned forward and waited.

"You're not a stupid girl," she said finally. "You have to know what Dom does... As you said, "who he is"."

I nodded, knowing it was dangerous to admit too much.

"I've been married to his father for twenty-six years now, and I can tell you first-hand how difficult it's been. Late nights, early mornings, days when I wondered if he'd come home at all... the lifestyle is lonely."

"I imagine."

"You imagine, but you don't know until you experience it. My father had no sons. Giovani—Dom's father—was his first soldier... the oldest of two orphans my father took in and raised as his own. Gio was loyal and ruthless, everything my father needed him to be. So when I came of age, Father arranged our marriage and made Gio a Mariani."

"Your marriage was arranged?" I asked, horrified.

"It's how things were done," she said with a wave of her hand. "How they're still done. There's no better way to form an alliance than with a marriage."

As her words sunk in, my mind drifted back to the girl in the pink dress who was bragging about marrying Dominico. My stomach sank. "Dom's marriage will be arranged, won't it? To the girl in the pink dress from the engagement party?"

"I see I don't need to explain much to you." She squeezed my hands. "That's helpful. You've met Valentina?"

It *was* true. My heart bottomed out as I leaned back in my chair. "No. Just overheard her in the bathroom. She's not right for Dom. She'll drive him crazy."

She nodded. "Gio never had the patience for puzzles. When we were children, he would force the pieces into place and get angry when they didn't form a picture. He hasn't changed much, still trying to force his pieces in where they don't belong. Everything would flow better if he took the time to find the right spot."

Dominico would have to marry Valentina. How long had he known? Since the party? Before? Had he been stringing me along this entire time? No, that didn't feel right. He loved me.

"He should have told me," I whispered, releasing Rosalie's hands to cradle my stomach. "I asked him about her and he…" What had he said? "Not if I have anything to say about it." What did that mean? Was Dominico plotting something to get out of marrying her? Cold dread filled my veins.

"What will happen if he disobeys his father?" I asked.

"Sharp as a tack," Rosalie replied, watching me. "I see why he likes you. He'll risk the wrath of his father, but that's a risk he's willing to take for you and his child."

Her vague answers were beginning to drive me crazy. The wrath of a don? What did that mean? "How much danger will he be in?" I asked.

"You let me take care of that," she said. "My grandbaby doesn't need the stress. But before I intervene, you have a decision to make. Do you want Dom enough to become a Mariani?"

Of course I did. I opened my mouth to tell her as much, but she stopped me.

"It's not as simple as it sounds. This is not an easy road to travel, and most people regret choosing it. You'll be lonely. Sure, you'll have your kids, friends, the family, knitting groups, book clubs, spa days, guard dogs you have to ditch in order to talk to your son's girlfriend, but none of them can ever truly know you. You can't show them weakness, can't talk about the family business, all relationships you have will be on the surface."

I frowned, letting her words sink in.

"Dom will buy you cars, clothes, jewelry, whatever you want. The only thing you won't have, is his time. He'll try to be there, but trust me... he'll miss birthdays, anniversaries, ball games, ballet recitals. Your children won't understand why he has to work all the time. Sometimes, even you will forget. One day, you'll get so frustrated and angry with him you'll be tempted to leave him. But make no mistake, Annetta, once you join this family, there is no walking away."

The cold, calculating Rosalie was back. She stared at me like she was waiting for something, but I had no idea what. Questions maybe? I had none. Everything she said, I'd already suspected. Did I love Dom enough to join him in his world? Did I love him enough to put him at risk so I could become a Mariani? I needed to think about it.

Her expression softened again. "You don't have to make any decisions today, dear. You have options. Should you decide you want out... that you want a normal marriage with a husband who can be there for you, Dom will survive. I will set you and the baby up somewhere safe, somewhere far away from here. You won't have any contact with my son, but you and the baby will be taken care of. You'll never have to worry about a thing."

"But I'll never see Dom again," I said, understanding what she meant. "And the baby will grow up without knowing him."

"It's unfortunate, but yes. If you decide this life isn't for you, Dom will have to move on. He still has duties, expectations, you understand."

I did understand. Dominico's mafia boss father would force him to marry that little tramp in the pink dress and I'd never see him again. "Yes ma'am."

She let out a breath, straightening her dress. "Good. Now let's put this unpleasantness behind us and enjoy the rest of our afternoon together. My grandchild needs a sweet, and the desserts here are to die for." She grabbed a menu from the table beside her and handed it to me. "I promise you will not be disappointed with anything, but the tiramisu is exquisite."

My appetite was gone, but Rosalie ordered us dessert anyway. As I nibbled, she spoke of a trip she'd recently taken to Italy, prattling on about scenic vineyards while my mind and heart churned about the problem at hand. Could I be in a relationship where I couldn't count on my other half to be home at night? The wives of truck drivers and undercover police officers did it all the time. I didn't need Dominico coddling me, and I knew not even the most attentive man would ever be responsible for my happiness. That was on me. And so far, I'd handled Dominico's absence pretty well. Soon I'd have the baby, and from what I'd read, my hands would be more than full. Especially if I planned to keep working. Which I did.

After dessert, Rosalie took me home. Before I exited her car, she grabbed my hand. "Think about your options, Annetta," she said. "Whatever you decide, I will help you. For the safety of you, Dom, and the baby, you will need to decide soon."

I nodded.

"Who have you told about the baby?"

"My best friend, Adona. That's it."

"Can you trust her not to tell anyone else?" she asked.

"Absolutely. I swore her to secrecy. She won't blab."

"You haven't told your father?"

Shame heated my cheeks. "No. I wanted to tell Dom first, and Papa got home late last night and left early this morning. I haven't had time." Also, I was a big chicken and didn't want to tell Papa I'd gotten knocked up.

"Good." She nodded to herself. "Tell no one. Not your father, your employer, no one. In fact, you need to quit your job."

Stunned, I stared at her, a protest forming on my lips.

"You must," Rosalie said, giving my hand a little squeeze. "I know you've worked hard and you love what you do, but you're beginning to show, and people will start asking questions. Dom has been careless in picking you up from work. The restaurant is connected. If they find out you're pregnant and suspect it's Dom's child, they'll tell Gio, which would be disastrous for all of us. Trust me on this, dear, he *will* kill you if he finds out before you're protected."

Strangely enough, I did trust her, but I was still devastated. Hand on my belly, I whispered, "I have to quit my job." Saying it aloud made it feel so final, so awful.

She nodded. "I know it will be difficult, but you can do it. Never underestimate what you can and will do for your child, Annetta. *Amor di madre, amore senza limiti.*"

A mother's love has no limits. Yes, I was beginning to see that. No doubt Rosalie was putting herself in danger by being here.

"Thank you for everything," I said, meaning it. "I just have one last question."

"Yes?"

"If I stay, are you sure you'll be able to keep the three of us safe?" It was the one key to the puzzle that I still didn't understand. Giovani sounded a little like the boogeyman, only he was very real. How could anyone protect us from him?

"Because I am a woman, my father wouldn't make me a capo. No family has ever had a female capo, and he refused to be the first. The old fool dreamed of taking Vegas, and believed he needed a strong male heir to turn that dream into reality. But Father never realized that women don't need a title to rule. The Mariani family will one day take Vegas, but it won't be because of the fear and respect my father demanded as a man and a capo. No, that earned him nothing but a pine box. You see, Annetta, real power doesn't need to demand fear and respect. When the Mariani family rises, it will be because strong women like us—the real power behind this family—got sick of watching our loved ones die and shoved our family to the top where it's harder for everyone to reach us."

She released my hand and passed me a piece of paper with a phone number written on it. "Take care of yourself and my grandbaby. That's my house number, but only use it from a payphone and in case of an emergency. Don't speak to anyone at this number but me."

I thanked her, and then headed into the house to think.

CHAPTER EIGHTEEN
Dominico

"GIVE HER A little time, Dom," Mamma said before sipping her wine.

Mamma had spent the day with Annetta before meeting up with me in a restaurant on the outskirts of Vegas to discuss a game plan. So far, the only plans my mother seemed to have involved waiting.

"I can't give her time," I replied. "If he finds out about her and the baby—" I gulped back the rest of the sentence, because I honestly had no idea what my father would do. Would he kill Annetta and our unborn child to keep them from getting in the way of his plans? Yes, I was certain he would. "You're sure she'll be safe if she agrees?"

Mamma nodded. "He can't kill her. Not unless he plans to kill you as well as all those loyal to the Mariani name. Gio forgets that he's not a Mariani by blood, but we all remember. He'll have to play the whole thing off like he knew about it and supported your decision, otherwise he'll look like a fool for letting you mess with his plans."

"And what about the Pelino family?" I asked.

"Adamo is a hothead. He'll be angry, no doubt. But he can't throw too big a fit, or your father will have to cut him off. As much as Adamo spoils Valentina, he won't risk his profits or his life for her. At least not without a better offer, which is a possibility. Adamo is not the faithful dog your father thinks he is."

"But will he cause problems?" I asked.

Mamma tapped the table. "Probably. The efforts to cripple the Durantes are going well. Money is pouring in right now, and we have the upper hand. I hope Adamo is smart enough not to let his ambition blind him. Gio will not tolerate any sort of an uprising right now. Your father has his faults, but he knows how to keep his men in line, Dom."

I blew out a breath, still unable to believe what we were planning, and afraid to put too much hope in the idea. Marrying Annetta! Was it really possible? Of course, there was another option Mamma and I weren't discussing. She'd given Annetta a way out. She wouldn't tell me the details, but if Annetta decides not to marry me, Mamma would help her take our son and disappear. The betrayal I feel over her making that offer stings.

"You should have let me talk to her first," I said, still upset by the way I'd been blackballed from their conversation.

"I needed to see for myself what she was made of," Mamma defended. "And this choice needs to be hers without any influence from you."

And it was tearing me up inside. What if she chose to walk away? Could I let her?

Mamma grabbed my hand. "Trust me, and trust her. This is a lot for both of you to take in. She'll need time to process, and you will, too. You can't just march in there and propose to her." She smiled. "As romantic as that sounds."

I'd never considered myself a goddamn romantic, but everything about Annetta made me want to get down on one knee and slide a fat rock onto her finger. Which reminded me I still needed to take care of that little detail. "You're right," I admitted. "I need to get a ring first."

"I've got it handled," Mamma said, pulling a small white box out of her pocket and setting it on the table. "This was my grandmother's. She was a strong woman, an anchor for my grandfather. I think she'd like Annetta and want her to have it."

Inside the box was a gorgeous round diamond on a unique vintage band. "Thank you," I said, admiring the ring. "It's perfect."

"And it will keep you out of jewelry stores. I do want you to wait a couple of days and let her think over everything first. You cannot push her into accepting this life, Dom."

Guilt pierced my chest. Annetta deserved more than a mobster for a husband, and I was a bastard for wanting to pluck her out of her safe, normal life and subject her to the dangers of my family. But with the baby coming, I didn't see any way around it. I had to marry her before Father found out about the baby. That is… if she'd have me.

"What if she says no?" I asked, fidgeting with the ring box in my pocket.

"She loves you." Mamma smiled reassuringly. "I'm already working on wedding arrangements, dear."

Relieved, I sat back down and swallowed back another gulp of beer, wishing it would chill me the fuck out. "Okay, I'll give her a couple of days."

"Good, because now we need to figure out where the two of you will live after the wedding."

*   *   *

Two days later I stood on Annetta's doorstep, clutching the ring in my pocket with a sweaty hand and clinging to the hope that the woman I loved wouldn't say no. I couldn't sleep, so I'd gotten up early and parked down the street, where I watched her father climb into his truck and take off for work. I wasn't afraid of her old man, but no matter what Annetta decided, I wanted it to be between me and her first.

She answered the door wearing a summer dress that hid her expanding belly, but not much else. My gaze traveled down the straps to her breasts, which were bulging against the fabric. The dress ended midthigh, showing off her perfect legs. Pregnancy looked good on her.

"You look amazing," I said.

Color crept up her cheeks as she patted her stomach. I'd never grow tired of seeing her blush... making her blush.

"I look fat, but thank you. Come in."

She stepped aside, and I walked in, closing the door behind me. Annetta started to walk away, but I caught her hand and spun her back around to face me. My nerves were going crazy, and I needed to taste her lips and reassure myself that this thing between was real. She opened her mouth to me and wrapped her hands around my waist, pulling me closer. Encouraged, I kissed her senseless before leading her to the sofa. Then, heart in my throat, I dropped to my knee, pulled out the little white box, and popped the question.

Annetta's eyes misted over as she looked from me to the ring. "This isn't about the baby, is it? I mean you want to marry *me*, right? I don't want you to feel obligated, because you don't have to—"

She was scared, worried, uncertain. Grabbing the back of her neck, I did my best to kiss those fears away. How could she question what I felt for her?

When we pulled apart, her gaze searched mine.

"I love you, Net, but I'd be lying if I said I wasn't grateful for this little peanut." My hands drifted to her stomach. "He kinda kicked my ass into gear and made me realize that I do want to marry you. Hell, I've thought about nothing else for the past three days."

She flashed me the most beautiful smile I'd ever seen before turning away. "It's so soon."

I grabbed the sides of her face and gently turned her to face me again. "Look, I know we haven't been together long, but you and me... We can do this. I know we can. Marry me. Please?"

Cheeks wet with tears and eyes full of trust, she nodded. "Yes. Okay. I will."

It was too good to be true, so I wrapped her in my arms and asked her to repeat herself.

She giggled. "Yes. I'll marry you, Dom."

Relieved, I knew just what I had to do. I stood, picking her up. She let out a little squeal as she leaned against me and settled in my arms.

"What are you doing?"

I headed for her bedroom. "I plan to make sure you don't change your mind."

She laughed. "Oh? And how do you plan on doing that?"

I pushed open her bedroom door and went in, gently lying Annetta on the bed. Pushing her dress up around her waist, I slowly slid her panties down her legs and flung them on the floor. Then, I leaned back and looked at her. She'd be my wife soon, but I'd never get tired of this view. Goddamn, she had great legs leading up to an hourglass figure, long neck, full lips, half-lidded eyes, and long dark hair. I wouldn't change a thing about her.

"You're so fuckin' beautiful."

"Sweet-talk, Dom?" she asked, shaking her head. "You're gonna need to do better than that to keep me."

"Keep talking, and I'll give you something constructive to do with that mouth."

Laughter danced in her eyes. She opened her mouth, but I cut off her reply when my lips landed on her clit. I kissed and blew before sucking and tonguing. Annetta writhed in pleasure beneath me, encouraging me to keep going. I licked and sucked for a while longer, enjoying the reaction of her body, until she started raising her hips, silently asking for more. She wanted more? I'd give it to her. Dipping two fingers into her wet pussy, I stroked her g-spot as my tongue flicked her clit.

"Oh god," she breathed, gripping the sheets at her sides.

I added a third finger and sucked her clit until she came. Then I replaced my fingers with my tongue, licking away her sweet wetness.

"I think you killed me," she said, her fingers still tangled in the sheets.

I chuckled. "I'm not done yet."

I stripped, and then, kissing my way up her curves, removed her dress and unfastened her bra. She'd had great tits before she got pregnant, but now... now I could get lost in them. Pinching one nipple, I sucked on the other as her hands released the sheets to roam over my back. My lips moved up to her collarbone as my hands played with her big, round breasts. I nibbled at her neck, sucked on her earlobe, and then brushed kisses against her jawline.

Annetta's lips parted, so I shifted my weight and kissed her deeply, letting her taste herself on my tongue as my hands roamed over her body before settling back down to play with her folds. Her wetness made me want to plunge my cock into her and fuck her until she screamed my name, but before I could, Annetta broke off the kiss.

"My turn," she whispered, pushing me off her.

Gladly relinquishing control, I laid back and watched her kiss her way down to my swollen dick. She rolled her tongue over the head and around the shaft, teasing. Watching me, she opened her mouth and slid me in, her lips closing around my shaft. She took me in deeper, until I felt the back of her throat, and then flicked her tongue up and down. I'd never encountered anyone who could challenge my control like she could. I moaned, struggling to hold back.

Her eyes sparkled with mischief and she picked up her pace, wrapping a hand around the base of my shaft while she fucked me with her mouth. Squeezing me with her hand, she continued. Knowing I was about to come, I tried to push her off, but she'd have none of it. She fucked me until I released into the back of her throat.

When my dick finally stopped throbbing, her mouth released me, but her hand stayed wrapped around my shaft. Eyes full of love and adoration, she stared up at me, and I was done for.

"I love you so damn much," I said.

"Good." Her hand drifted down to give my balls a little squeeze. "But I'm gonna need you to get hard again so you can convince me to marry you with more than your tongue."

I chuckled. Not only was she beautiful, but I'd turned her into a freak. My freak. How the fuck had I gotten so lucky?"

"You already said yes," I reminded her.

She licked my shaft from balls to tip, smiling seductively at me.

"What's wrong, Dom. Scared of a little challenge?"

Her sassy mouth and hot body already had me growing hard again. "Why don't you get on your hands and knees and I'll show you just how scared I am."

She did as she was told, and I grabbed her hips and buried myself deep inside her. Reaching around to play with her clit, I fucked her until we both came again. Then I held her and watched her sleep. Mario was covering for me today, because I refused to leave her side until I had a conversation with her old man.

*　　*　　*

Just a handful of days after Annetta agreed to marry me, I stood beside the priest and watched her walk down the aisle on the arm of her smiling father. She wore a vintage white dress and all I could think about was getting her out of it. The wedding was quick and small, with only my mother, Annetta's father, Mario, Adona, and the priest in attendance. We said the customary words, followed the traditions Mother insisted on, kissed, and then were announced as Mr. and Mrs. Dominico Mariani.

She deserved so much more, but I couldn't give it to her. At least, not yet. We'd done it, though. Annetta had my name, and Mamma promised that Annetta Mariani and our child would be safe... even from my father. I'd never felt more happy and relieved in my life as I did when we left the church and she climbed into the passenger seat of my car.

Because I no longer cared about discretion, I bypassed our usual room at the Davenport and booked the honeymoon suite at the Caribbean, one of the neutral casinos. We'd barely checked in when Father and Michael burst through the door.

"Annetta?" Michael asked, his eyes wide with shock as he took her in. "The cook from the restaurant?"

The look she gave me told me she couldn't believe I hadn't told my brother about us. To him, she said, "It's nice to see you again, Michael."

Father stepped forward and introduced himself, hugging Annetta and kissing her cheeks, very publicly accepting her. She had to be confused. Mamma and I had told her Father and Michael couldn't make it to the wedding because of work, yet here they were.

"Welcome to the family, daughter," he said.

She glanced at me before smiling at him. "Thank you. We missed you at the wedding. I was sad to hear that you were detained with work."

He frowned. "Me too. But that's why we're here. We have some business requiring Dom's assistance. I apologize for stealing him away on your wedding night, but it cannot be helped. We'll have him back before morning, and he can take tomorrow off."

Annetta looked to me, her eyes full of questions.

"Please let me take her up to the room," I said.

Father nodded, the warmth he'd shown Annetta disappearing. "Be quick."

Annetta opened her mouth to protest, but I ushered her into the elevator. The moment the doors were closed, she turned on me.

"But we just got married," she protested. "Don't we get one night?"

"I know. I'm sorry, Net. Something important must have come up."

But I couldn't think of a single thing they'd need me to handle. This had to be some sort of power play to put me in my place. No doubt, I was about to get punished for my misstep. It didn't matter. At least he'd accepted Annetta. She and our child would be protected no matter what.

"I'm sure it won't take long, but why don't you call Mamma and have her come sit with you. Maybe the two of you could watch a movie or something."

The elevator doors opened, but she made no move to follow me out.

"This is my wedding night, Dom. I don't want to watch movies with your mom."

And I didn't want to go defend my decision to my father. I closed the distance between us and kissed her, tugging her into the hall with me. "You think I want you to?"

When she still refused to move, I picked her up and carried her into our room. Setting her on the bed, I checked the room to reassure myself it was empty. It was dangerous to keep my old man waiting, and I was already in enough trouble, so I kissed her one last time before hurrying out to see what he wanted.

Father didn't say one word as we piled into his Cadillac. He drove northeast on Highway 147 until we were outside the city, turned down a dirt road, and killed the engine. We all got out of the car and Father handed us each a cigar.

"In celebration of your child," he said.

Wondering if I'd somehow managed to dodge a bullet, I smoked a cigar with my old man and brother as we discussed the recent Dodgers game. My old man had always been a baseball fan, but this shit felt surreal. It was like Father wanted me to think he and I were cool, when I knew we weren't.

When we stomped out our cigars, everything changed. Father gestured at me, and said, "Michael, your brother's stepped out of line. Set him straight."

Knowing better than to block him or to fight back, I stood there as Michael punched me in the stomach until I folded over. Then he kneed me in the face. Stars danced in my vision. He backed up and punched me in the side, and then swiped my legs out from under me with a kick. When I hit the ground, he rolled me onto my back and started working over my stomach again.

I knew my brother didn't want to hurt me, but he'd learned long ago not to pull his punches. The old man could always tell. By the time Father told him to stop, I could barely get off the ground. The two of them returned to Father's car and drove off, leaving me alone in the dark.

It hurt to even breathe, but I managed to pull myself up and start limping back the way we'd come. After all, I had a bride to get to, and at least the bastards had left me alive.

CHAPTER NINETEEN
Dominico

*A*NNETTA HAD BEEN spitting mad when I finally showed up, beaten and bloody, the morning after we got married. She'd spent most of the night on the phone with Mamma, and the moment I limped through the door, she made sure I was okay and then demanded an explanation. Since I didn't have the energy to dissuade her, I redirected her, requesting a medical kit and some pain killers.

"Okay, but this isn't over," she said, heading out of the hotel room.

I laid on the bed and promptly passed out.

I must have slept through the day and night, because the next time I awoke it was morning again. Bruised and sore, but able to move again, I checked us out of the hotel and we drove to the newly-built four-bedroom house I'd closed on the day before.

Every inch of my body hurt, but it didn't stop me from carrying my beautiful bride over the threshold, despite her many and loud objections. Finally, she stopped trying to wiggle free and just relaxed against me.

"This doesn't mean I forgive you," she said.

"For getting beat up?"

"Yes. Next time, you kick their ass."

Chuckling, I kissed her forehead and set her down in the stone entryway.

"Welcome home, Net."

She gasped, her eyes wide as she spun around. "We're living here?"

Before I could answer, she tugged me behind her to check the place out.

It was a nice house. Two stories, thick carpet for the baby to crawl on, a fireplace we could make love in front of, big bedrooms with walk-in-closets, a master suite with a jetted tub, a swimming pool in the back yard, clean and bright, but nothing too lavish. It was also completely empty.

"We bought it," I said, handing her a key. "It's ours, Net."

Her eyes were still wide. "Doesn't it take like a month to buy a house? How did you pull this off?"

Cash could close a loan unbelievably quick. "Mamma warned you about the dangers, but didn't fully detail the perks." I tried to smile but ended up wincing at the pain in my cheek.

"She definitely forgot to mention the beating you'd get on our wedding night."

I'd told Annetta that I got jumped while on a job. I was pretty sure she didn't buy it, but luckily, I'd talked her out of trying to hunt down my attackers, at least for now. We need a topic change before she started asking questions again.

"I was gonna get furniture, but Mamma said you should be the one picking it out."

Annetta halted her exploration long enough to stare up at me, her eyes once again full of happiness and passion. "If you weren't a mess of bruises, I'd attack you right now," she said.

"What's a little pain for a shit-ton of pleasure?" I asked.

Rolling her eyes, she smiled and tugged me along to finish exploring our house.

*   *   *

Annetta spent the next couple of months preparing for the baby, buying furniture, and turning our home into a happy place, full of laughter, music, and comforting food smells. I cherished every moment I got to spend with her there, unfortunately, they were few and far between. Our attack on the Durantes was still in full swing, and we were gaining ground.

Much to my amusement, Annetta's friend, Adona, was still hot for Mario. Wanting to see my shy, no-game-havin' friend squirm, we threw together a dinner for four and invited them both. Mario walked in, took one look at Adona wearing a low-cut dress and come-hither look, and immediately turned to bolt. Sensing that my friend could use a little help, I stepped in front of him and closed the door.

He looked betrayed, but I had a sneaking suspicion he'd get over it.

"Enjoy," I said, walking past Adona.

"Oh, I plan to," she said, on the prowl toward her prey.

The night must not have been too bad, because they left together, and had been dating ever since.

As Annetta got further along, Mamma took over one of the spare bedrooms, so she could be there when the baby came. Knowing Mamma had things under control freed me up to focus on my job. I was helping the family move a couple of televisions which had "fallen off a truck" on the crisp February morning I got the page I'd been waiting for. I called the house and Mamma told me Annetta was in labor.

"These things take time, Dom. Sometimes even days," Mamma informed me when I called in. "I'm taking her to the hospital and I'll page you again when you need to come."

Mamma paged me four hours later, and I barely made it in time to robe up and cut the umbilical cord. Born healthy and with a powerful cry, D'Angelo had a full head of dark curls and the tiniest hands and feet I'd ever seen. I was the first to hold him, terrified I'd drop him or squeeze him too tightly. When I handed him off to Annetta, the way she looked at him made my life feel complete. We'd done it. We'd beaten the odds and found some measure of freedom inside my father's world. I didn't think I'd ever be happier, but life got even better.

The day after Angel's birth, the Commission and their messaggero negotiated the families into a ceasefire. We were so close to taking down the Durantes that Father grumbled nonstop. I, on the other hand, couldn't wait to spend more time with my wife and child. As I drove them home from the hospital, I reflected on how great my luck had been.

As soon as we got home, Mamma took the baby and ordered me to put my wife to bed, insisting that Annetta needed some sleep. She didn't even protest as I picked her up, carried her to our room, and laid her on the bed. I started pulling down her pants, and she laughed.

"I'm not helpless, you know."

"I know you're not." I kissed her leg and tugged her pants over her feet. "But you just gave me one hell of a cute kid. I can show you my gratitude."

Once we were both naked, I snuggled in beside her, thinking my life couldn't get any better.

Four weeks later I got the page that changed everything.

I was in the middle of a weapons exchange when our home phone number flashed across my pager. Annetta rarely reached out to me while I was at work, so I peeled off shortly after the deal to give her a ring.

"Dom," she breathed, sounding like she'd been crying.

"What's wrong?" I asked, instantly on alert. "Is the baby okay?"

"Who the fuck is Tiffany?" she asked.

Shocked to hear her swear, I wracked my brain, trying to remember a Tiffany. "I don't know. Who is she?"

"Don't play dumb with me."

"Annetta, I'm not. I promise you, I don't know a Tiffany."

"Well she sure as hell knows you. She said she couldn't deal with the guilt anymore.. not now that we have a kid... so she had to tell me you've been sleeping together."

What the fuck? Now I was getting pissed. "I swear to god, I don't know any goddamn Tiffany," I said.

"The Davenport Hotel, room 325. Said you meet her there. If you don't know this girl, how does she know about our room, Dom?"

Good question. My shoulders tensed as I made a mental note to go visit my night clerk friend and find out who he'd told. "I don't know. Someone's fuckin' with me."

"You need to tell me if you're sleeping with her," Annetta said, sounding devastated. "I know I haven't been able to do anything lately because of Angel, but I thought you were okay with that. If you're not happy, you should have told me."

She didn't believe me. After all we'd been through, it felt like a slap in the face. "Would you listen to me for a goddamn minute?" I asked. "I don't know this Tiffany bitch, and I'm definitely not cheating on you. If I had time to fuck anyone, I'd be home in our bed. You should know me better than that."

"I don't know, Dom," she sobbed. "I don't know anything right now."

Someone was messing with us while she was tired and jacked up on pregnancy hormones. When I found out who, I'd kill the dumbass.

"Where's Mamma?" I asked.

"She went to the store a little while ago."

"Perfect goddamn timing," I grumbled. "Net, I swear there is no Tiffany. There is nobody else. I love you. You know this."

"I do, Dom, but she knew things. She talked about the tub."

How the fuck? That desk clerk had some serious explaining to do. "I'll be home as soon as I can," I promised her before hanging up.

A quick glance at my watch told me I had only a half hour before the pick up at the Pelino warehouse, but I needed to get home. Now. I paged Michael, sending him the number of the payphone. He called me back within minutes, and I explained the situation, asking him to handle the Pelino pickup.

"Dom—" Michael started.

Hearing the disapproval in his voice, I stopped him. "I know the Pelinos are my responsibility. I'm sorry, Mike. I wouldn't ask you if this wasn't important. Pregnancy hormones are no joke."

Michael chuckled. He and Zeta were expecting a child in a few months, so I knew he'd sympathize. "Okay, but you owe me one."

"Whatever you want," I promised before hanging up.

Breaking multiple speed laws, I got home in record time, only to find a strange car in the driveway and the front door wide open. Drawing my pistol, I clicked off the safety and crept inside. The living room was quiet and still. Nobody in the kitchen. I thought about calling out to Annetta, but if anyone was here, I didn't want to alert them to my presence.

Creeping down the hall, I searched each room until I reached ours. Turning the doorknob, I pulled open the door and stepped aside. Gun outstretched, I peered in.

"Dom?" Annetta asked, sounding both scared and hopeful.

I stepped into the room. Holding Angel, she sat huddled in the corner, her eyes swollen and a gun in her hand. Two steps away from the door lay the crumpled over body of a man I didn't recognize, surrounded by bloody carpet.

"You okay?" I asked, pointing my pistol at the body. It wasn't moving.

"He was gonna hurt Angel," she said. "I didn't have a choice. I got your gun out of the nightstand and—"

Her hands were trembling. I hurried over and took the gun, flicking on the safety and hiding it back in the nightstand. Then I wrapped her and Angel in a hug, picking them up and moving them to the bed.

"You're both okay?" I asked. "Nobody's hurt?"

Annetta relaxed her arms so I could see Angel. He was sleeping soundly. Relieved, I let out a breath.

"You did great, Net." I sat behind her and pulled her against my chest. "You're safe now. Tell me what happened."

"I don't know," she said as tears slid down her cheeks. "After that awful phone call, I called you. I was so upset I... I went to check on Angel." She glanced at the bassinet beside our bed. "When I turned around, that man was standing in the doorway, pointing his gun at me. Said he needed to take the baby. I couldn't let him do that, Dom."

"Shhhh." I kissed her forehead. "I know you couldn't. You protected him. You did the only thing you could do."

"I... It's a mess. I don't know what to do with the body," she said. "I want it out of my house, but I didn't know who to call."

"I'll take care of it," I said, reaching for the phone on the nightstand. "It will be okay."

"I... Do you think this is connected to that call from Tiffany?" she asked.

I squeezed her against me. "I don't know, baby, but I'll get to the bottom of it. I promise."

Little did I know, our house was only one of the hits made that night.

CHAPTER TWENTY
Dominico

FATHER WAS DEAD. Try as I might, I could not reconcile the hard-as-nails, mean-ass man who'd raised me with the corpse laid out in the pine box. The Durantes had finally gotten him. He'd been heading into Antonio's for a meeting when they'd taken him down. Of course, my old man didn't go down alone; he made sure drag Maurizio to hell with him.

Michael should have been dead as well. Taking my place at the Pelino pickup, had earned him two bullets in the spine. Then he shot Adamo and two more of his men, buying our soldiers enough time to pull him out of there and rush him to the hospital. So far, my brother had undergone three surgeries. The bullets had been removed, but the doctors said he'd never walk again. Michael would spend the rest of his life in a wheelchair.

"Dom," Carlo said by way of greeting, joining me at the casket.

"What have you heard from the messaggero?" I asked, still staring down at my old man's lifeless form.

"The hit was unprovoked and unsanctioned. The Commission gave us the thumbs-up to retaliate, and we hit them this morning."

"This morning?" I asked, stunned. "I should have been there. Why didn't anyone tell me?"

He laid a hand on my shoulder. "Because as soon as this shit's over, the family will swear allegiance to you. You'll be our new capo. We couldn't risk you."

Confused, I stared at him. "But Michael will recover. He's the heir."

"The men won't follow a cripple," Carlo said frankly. "They need strength right now, and they're willing to pledge to you."

Still reeling, I asked, "How did the hit go?"

"We got all the Durantes except Joey. The little bastard slipped through our fingers."

Joey Durante was Maurizio's youngest son. "He's just a baby, isn't he?" I asked.

"As your father always reminded us, babies grow up to be men, thirsty for revenge."

Yeah, but the old man was dead. "I'm not my father, Carlo."

"I'm aware."

He sounded disappointed. No doubt, they all were.

"What about Gino?" I asked.

"No sign of him."

Carlo was holding back something.

"When's the last time he checked in?"

"Two weeks ago. They might have discovered him, Dom."

My world was crumbling around me. Father was dead, Michael was crippled, and Gino was probably dead. At least they'd taken our enemies with them.

"And the Pelinos?" I asked.

"Found them holed up with the Durantes... all except Ciro and his kid."

Valentina's big brother was still roaming the streets. No doubt that would come back to bite us in the ass long before Maurizio's baby did.

Carlo finished his report and excused himself to talk to one of his cousins.

I went through the rest of the funeral in a daze, shaking hands and thanking people for coming the way I'd been trained to do. They looked at me different now, like the death of my old man and the crippling of my brother had turned me into a goddamn king. I didn't want any of it, but whenever I'd start looking for the exits, my gaze would find Annetta. Seated in the second pew, holding our sleeping child, her reassuring smile gave me the strength to keep going.

When the funeral wrapped up, Annetta and I followed the hearse to the graveside to lay my old man to rest. As he was lowered six feet under, I knew I should feel something, but all I felt was cold. Buttoning my coat, I reflected on the man in the box. The bastard had never been much of a father to me. I couldn't imagine forcing Angel to beat the shit out of his younger brother while I stood there and watched. What the fuck was wrong with him? Determined to do better—to be better—I tucked my wife and son under my arm. *We* would be different.

After the graveside service, we headed to my parents' house for a family potluck. Homemade dishes of every sort covered the bar and table as people huddled in groups, talking about my old man like he was some sort of legend. I drifted around the room, catching stories of his exploits. He'd stolen a cop car, peed on an electric fence, botched a robbery, got so drunk he passed out naked in a night club. The man they spoke of sounded fun and a little wild. I wish I could have known him, rather than the asshole I'd grown up fearing.

As the potluck came to an end, women collected their dishes as the men approached me. The first of which, was Mamma's cousin Gus. Gus had to be approaching his seventies, which made him a relic among mobsters.

"It was a respectable service," he said, shaking my hand. "Thank you for coming, Gus." I replied. "It was good to see you and your family. It's been too long."

When was the last time I'd seen Gus? He hadn't come to Michael or Abriana's weddings. When I'd become a made man, maybe?

"We don't get out much anymore. Rarely see a reason for it." He leaned closer and lowered his voice. "I don't mean to speak ill of the dead, but I never much cared for your old man. He wasn't a Mariani, and never should have been leading this family."

Stunned, I held my tongue.

"But you... You're a Mariani, son, and I have all the confidence in the world you'll do everything you can to see this family prosper." He clapped me on the back. "That's what Marianis do. You need anything, you come and see me, you hear?"

I said the only thing I could think of. "Thank you, Gus."

He smiled and walked away.

Mamma's cousin Manuel came next, and basically told me the same thing. Manuel was followed by Luca, after Luca, came Allessio, as Allessio left, a line formed. Every single man shook my hand, revealed their dislike for my father, and assured me I'd do better.

By the time I packed Annetta and Angel into the car and drove away from Mamma's, there was no doubt in my mind that the family had accepted me as the new capo, a job I'd never wanted but was now stuck with. Looking for advice, I dropped Annetta and Angel off at home and went to the hospital to visit Michael.

Although this wasn't my first visit, it still stunned me to see my brother lying in bed and hooked to machines. He smiled when he saw me, shooing away the nurse who was taking his vitals.

"How was the service?" he asked once we were alone.

"Respectable." At least that's what everyone had called it.

Michael chuckled, no doubt understanding why I'd used that word.

"How are you feeling?" I asked.

"Feeling? They got me hopped up on so much dope I can't feel a damn thing. I pissed myself earlier. Didn't even feel it."

I laughed, glad to see him in such good spirits.

"How's Zeta taking it?" I asked.

"Honestly? I think she's relieved."

"Relieved?" I asked, surprised. "You'll never be able to walk again."

"Yeah, but I'll be home at night now. She said she's looking forward to that, especially with the baby on the way."

I sat in the chair beside my brother's bed. This was the first time we'd been alone since the accident and I had so much to say to him, but no clue how to start. I used to be able to tell Michael anything, but over the past few years, he'd turned into my boss rather than my brother. Now he was lying in the bed Adamo Pelino had intended for me, forced to be my brother again.

"I'm sorry," I said. "I know I can't ever make up for it, but I'm sorry I asked you to go to the Pelinos that night. It was my responsibility."

"You didn't shoot me, Dom," Michael replied.

"Yeah, but had I gone—"

"Then maybe you'd be dead, and you sure as shit wouldn't have been able to nail Adamo between the eyes like I did. You're nowhere near as good a shot as me."

"You're full of shit." I leaned back in my chair. "Remember that Christmas we got those pellet guns? I gave you so many welts Mamma thought you had chicken pox."

He laughed.

I couldn't remember the last time I'd joked with Michael. It felt good. Maybe I should steal a few bottles of whatever they were giving him so I could dope him up the next time he turned into an asshole.

When his laughter died, silence stretched between us once more. I waited, trying to build up the courage to say what I needed to say, but before I could, Michael spoke.

"I'll help you, Dom. I can't walk, but I'm still me. I've been training for this shit my entire life, and I know what the hell I'm doing. You'll need me."

Relieved, I let out a deep breath. "Thanks, man."

"I mean sure, you've got the legs, but I'm the brains. You'd be screwed without me."

A smile tugged at my lips. "Want me to break your arms too?"

Ignoring me, he continued. "You'll also have Uncle Carlo, the cousins, second cousins, third cousins, Mamma, hell, you could even call Bri."

"You think I'll need that much help, huh?"

"Abso-fuckin'-lutely."

I chuckled. "Thanks Mike. By the way, I don't know what they've got you on, but you're obviously high."

"Hmm?" he asked.

"You didn't nail Adamo between the eyes. You got him in the right cheek. You're lucky you were on the ground and the bullet angled up through his brain, otherwise he would have gotten away."

"Bullshit. I didn't shoot him in the cheek."

"You did too."

"Prove it. Show me a picture."

"Do I look like a goddamn photographer? Even if I was, I sure as hell wouldn't be taking photos of Adamo's ugly ass!"

"Don't act like you've never taken a picture of a corpse before."

Shaking my head at the memory of when we'd been young, dumb, and daring, I said, "That was different. I was ten, there was a reward, and you dared me to break into that morgue. Never again."

"Chicken shit." Michael coughed around the word.

"You're such an ass," I said.

"Yeah, but you're glad I'm not dead."

He had me there. I nodded. "Thanks for not dying, Mike."

"No fuckin' Pelino can knock off a Mariani. Carlo told me Father finally took down Maurizio."

I chuckled. Like a goddamn coward, Maurizio had popped our old man in the back. Then the son-of-bitch was stupid enough to walk up on Father, and gloat over his corpse. It was the last mistake the Durante capo would ever make.

"What's that thing the old man always said when we were training?" Michael asked.

"Two in the head, make sure he's dead."

"Yeah. Bet Maurizio's wishin' someone would have told him that right about now. Two in the head, bastard, make sure he's dead. Fuckin' sloppy. I don't know how the hell he took Vegas in the first place."

I thought Maurizio was more cocky than sloppy, but was just glad to be rid of the lunatic.

"You ever find out who called Annetta and told her you were sleepin' around?"

"Nope. I tracked the desk clerk to his apartment, but someone had slit his throat and left him to rot. Carlo pulled some strings at the telephone company, but the number came from a payphone downtown."

"Whoever it was, you'll get 'em, Dom," He said.

Before I could reply, he started talking about another crazy thing we did as kids.

Thankful for the painkillers that had brought my brother back—if only for a while—I stayed at Michael's bedside, swapping memories until he drifted off to sleep.

CHAPTER TWENTY-ONE
Annetta

*I*T WAS ALMOST ten p.m. by the time Dominico stumbled through the front door of our house. Knowing exactly what he'd need after the day he'd had, I tugged off my robe, revealing sexy babydoll lingerie, and waited for him in the living room.

Dom entered with his head down, like he bore the weight of the world on his shoulders. Without seeing me, he removed his suit jacket and tossed it over the back of the sofa.

"Rough day?" I asked, flicking on the fireplace.

When his gaze found me, his jaw dropped. "Damn," he said.

The way he still looked at me—a mix of love and hunger, almost like he wanted to eat me up—made my skin tingle and my heart race. I'd been stupid to believe that Tiffany bitch, and if I ever found her, I'd rip every single strand of her hair out. This thing between me and Dominico... nobody would interfere with.

"You look incredible." Dom closed the distance between us, wrapping his arms around me.

I slid my hands between our chests and started unbuttoning his shirt.

"What's going on?" he asked.

Once his shirt was open, I undid his cufflinks, tugged his shirt off, and tossed it on the coffee table. "You look warm, so I'm helping you cool down."

He chuckled. "I'm pretty sure you're heating me up."

I smiled innocently. "It's practically the same thing."

He kicked off his shoes. I unbuttoned his pants and slid them over his already growing cock. Then I dropped to my knees, pulled down his boxers, and shoved him in my mouth.

Dominico gasped.

Since he wasn't fully hard, I took him all in, tickling the back of my throat with this throbbing head until he was fully erect. Then I slid my mouth up and down his shaft and played with his balls for a while, thoroughly enjoying myself. Although I was having fun, my man needed more, to let off some steam, so I placed his hands on the back of my head and encouraged him to let loose. Understanding what I wanted him to do, Dominico gripped by head and began fucking my mouth. Opening wider, I grabbed his ass and held on.

"Fuck," he hissed.

I nodded. Yep, that's what I wanted him to do.

The next time he plunged his dick into my mouth, I started humming.

Moaning, he threw back his head and closed his eyes.

I kept humming until hot come hit the back of my throat. Then I licked him clean and sat him on the sofa, straddling him.

"You sure know how to welcome a guy home," he said with a grin.

"Not just any guy," I replied. "My capo."

He studied me, brushing my hair back. "And you're all right with this?"

"Honestly, I wish you didn't have to do it," I replied. "But we're a part of this family, and there is no getting out. Somebody has to lead us. Who better than you?"

My question seemed to catch him off guard. He had to think about it for a moment before announcing, "Carlo."

I shook my head. "Not a Mariani. Besides, I don't trust him. Something about Carlo is... off."

"Gus."

"Too old."

"Luca."

I leveled a stare at him. "Are you even being serious right now?"

"What's wrong with Luca?"

"You said yourself he was lazy."

He kept watching me. "You really think I can do this?"

Nodding, I replied, "You have to."

"I know. I just... This could put you and Angel in greater danger. I can't do that."

"Then don't," I said, kissing his neck.

"You make it sound so easy."

"That day your mother took me out, she told me that the family would be the safest when it controlled Vegas. When we reach the top, it will be harder for the other families to reach us. I didn't fully understand what she was saying then, but now I do. With the Durantes and the Pelinos out of the picture, you can take this city and control it. You're a natural protector, Dom. This is your chance to build an empire that will keep us all safe. You can create balance and establish some level of order among the families. Mamma and I have been talking to the wives of the other families, and—"

"You have?" he asked. "When did you have time to do that?"

"When they started calling here after your father died. They're all sick of the fighting and have convinced their husbands to sit down with you and talk. They want order, Dom. They want peace, so they can go about their business and make money."

"You know what this is gonna take, right?" he asked.

"Yes." I trailed kisses across his pecks. "You'll have to lead with an iron fist. Not like your father, but like... I don't know. Some badass capo who doesn't take shit from anyone."

He chuckled. "I'm already a badass capo who doesn't take shit from anyone."

"Oh yeah?" I asked, sliding his cock up between my legs to rub it against my clit. "Prove it."

"Careful with that," he warned. "You might start something you can't finish."

"The doctor cleared me during my appointment yesterday," I said, still playing with his cock.

"What?! And you didn't tell me?"

I rocked my hips back and forth. "You should have come home before midnight."

That dangerous, enticing glint I loved so much was back in his eyes. "What are you clear to do?" He nuzzled my neck and slipped the straps of lingerie over my shoulders to expose my breasts. "Anything? Everything?"

I arched my back until my nipples rubbed against his bare chest, enjoying the contact. "Anything and everything."

"I love you so damn much." He slid his cock inside me with a moan. "And I missed the fuck outta this pussy."

Turned out, it had missed him too. Being on his lap put me a little over eye level with Dom. Gripping his shoulders for support, I slid up and down his cock, taking him deeper and deeper inside me while our tongues danced. He let me ride him for a while before bending me over the arm of the sofa and taking me from behind. While he reached around to finger my clit, his left hand slapped my ass, intensifying the pleasure.

"Am I enough of a badass for you now?" he asked.

"I don't know, do it again."

He laughed and spanked me again before he turned me around, propping my ass on the arm of the sofa. He lifted my legs in the air, holding me by the ankles as he plunged into me again. It felt so good I wanted to lie back and close my eyes, but Dominico made me look at him until we both came.

Afterward, he carried me to bed and climbed in beside me.

"I love you," he said, his gaze heavy with lust and love.

"I know." I kissed his lips and scooted closer to him. "I love you too."

In the silence that stretched between us, I could almost hear him thinking. And then, just as I was beginning to drift to sleep, he spoke.

"Schedule the meeting with the other families." Brushing my hair back with his fingers, he kissed my forehead. "We're gonna build an empire, Net."

Thank you so much for reading **Dom's Ascension**. I hope you've enjoyed the journey and will check out some of my other books. Please help support my work by writing a review on Amazon. Reviews only require twenty words and help me tremendously. I appreciate your support!

Also, be sure to visit my website and sign up to be included on news about future releases:
http://www.harleystoneauthor.com

Find me on Facebook, too!
https://www.facebook.com/HarleyStoneAuthor/

Coming soon from Harley Stone:

Dial A for Addison: S.A.F.E. Detective Agency #1
Throw Dylan from the Train: S.A.F.E. Detective Agency #2
Making Angel: Mariani Crime Family Book 2
Breaking Bones: Mariani Crime Family Book 3

Made in United States
Orlando, FL
13 June 2023

34121708R00104